MEN ARE LIKE STREET CARS

"Do you suppose," I said, "that I haven't been awakened?"

MEN ARE LIKE
STREET CARS

BY GRAEME *and* SARAH LORIMER

WITH ILLUSTRATIONS BY MARGE

Short Story Index Reprint Series

BOOKS FOR LIBRARIES PRESS
FREEPORT, NEW YORK

First Published 1932
Reprinted 1970

STANDARD BOOK NUMBER:
8369-3563-2

LIBRARY OF CONGRESS CATALOG CARD NUMBER:
78-122730

PRINTED IN THE UNITED STATES OF AMERICA

TO

HUNTER
AND HIS CROWD

CONTENTS

ILLUSTRATIONS

MEN ARE LIKE STREET CARS

I

WHAT EVERY GIRL SHOULD NO

It's certainly interesting, what two years can do to a person. Here was Lysbeth, a high bicycle at fourteen if ever there was one, and now holding everybody around the table positively spellbound. Why, they couldn't even eat.

"A crush party!" Pauline said. "My goodness, what's a crush party?"

"Well, honestly!" Lysbeth said. "How perfectly quaint! Didn't you any of you ever have a crush party with any of the boys around here?"

"No," said Julie Purviance in a sort of reverent tone, "what is it?"

3

Lysbeth tried to smile pityingly with her mouth full. "Why, my dear, how simply sobbing," she said. "Imagine not knowing what a crush party is! What do you think men are for?"

Julie still looked dumb, which it wasn't a very hard thing for her to do.

"Good grief, do I have to go into details and draw a diagram and everything?" Lysbeth said, lighting one of father's cigarettes and blowing smoke all over everybody with an air of disdain. "You innocent children make me feel positively antique."

Well, I just wished Mother could hear, that was all. All through the years, up to the time I was fourteen, I had to listen to Mother saying what a suitable companion for me Lysbeth was — just the picture of her mother at her age — and wear myself out giving her a good time when she came to visit, which I would have to go around and make it up to everybody for, after she left. Mother and Lysbeth's mother were dear friends all through their childhood, so they seemed to feel they had to sick me and Lysbeth onto each other. Then her family moved so far away we couldn't visit for a couple of happy years, but now they were back in sicking distance again and in a fit of friendship Mother had invited Lysbeth for over Thanksgiving. Well, I bet Mother was going to cool off some

4

about dear Caroline's darling daughter when she saw how she got lipstick all over the napkins.

"Do you actually mean to say you let Chi kiss you the first time you met him?" Pauline asked in shocked tones.

"Kiss me!" Lysbeth laughed loudly. "That boy should be on the wrestling team."

It looked like Lysbeth had turned into one of these younger generation you're always hearing about.

"But I don't see how — " Julie looked quite puzzled. "You didn't know Chi before you came here, did you?"

"No, darling," Lysbeth said; "I never laid eyes on him before last night. But I think he's awfully cute."

"Not as cute as Davy, do you think, Pauly?" Julie said to Pauline, as one friend to another.

"Oh, cuter," Pauline said. I smiled quietly to myself. I own Davy Dillon. He's really awfully cute.

"But I don't see how — " Julie said, like a dog coming back to a bone — "how you get intimate like that with a boy when you've just met him. I should think a nice boy like Chi — "

"They're all alike, nice ones and all," Lysbeth gave us her superior smile, "when you stir up the old B. U."

"B. U.?" Julie asked dumbly. B. U. is so old it's been called in around here, but trust Julie — honestly that girl has moths in the piano.

"Why, biological urge, of course, darling," Lysbeth said. "And I have a way that never fails."

"You have?" Pauline was all ears. "How?" I felt disappointed in Pauline. That was just what Lysbeth had wanted somebody to ask.

"Don't be dull," Lysbeth blew smoke through her nose in a very sophisticated manner; "you don't expect me to give away my system to you, when it's taken me years to develop it?" I suppose a person ought to observe the duties of hospitality to a guest and all, but that woman of the world line from Lysbeth, who I happen to know is three days younger than I am, was just too much. And besides, a person can't help having some ideals and morals.

I swept Lysbeth with a haughty look. "We don't call petting a system around here. We just call it petting. That is, we did call it petting. It's sort of gone out now — it's sort of a little old-fashioned. I mean, we sort of think a system means being a little clever and I don't see anything very clever in being a sausage."

Lysbeth looked rather blank. The ice cream was around to me and I was trying to get some chocolate without any of the green. I loathe green food.

"What's a sausage?" Julie said.

"Anybody's meat," I said, still working on the ice cream. Lysbeth looked mad, as who wouldn't? Julie looked awfully dazed, but Pauline, who had been shut up practically every time she tried to say anything, leaped in happily.

"Maudie," she said, "I suppose Davy's taking you to the Paint and Powder next Friday, isn't he? Gosh, Maudie, this green end is like soup. I ought to have a straw. Gosh! Well, anyhow, is he?"

Before I could tell her, and I wasn't going to anyhow, Lysbeth boiled over.

"I suppose you think you're the girl of the U. S. A. or something?" Lysbeth said in a mean way. Julie and Pauline laughed a smothered laugh.

"Not at all," I said. "That's what I'm trying to tell you. I have a system that is a system, that takes brains, not muscle."

"Brains?" Lysbeth said, making an unattractive noise. "That gets a laugh out of me before you begin."

"I'm not beginning," I said. "I've ended. Your way may be perfectly all right for you, but I think it's lousy. My system gets me what I want out of boys and I don't get my hair mussed either." I was feeling rather fed up in more ways than one. "Are you all ever going to stop eating? Because it's after two — "

7

Lysbeth cut in, knocking my sentence down my throat till I about choked. "The thing about you is, Maudie," she said, glowering down at me as we went into the hall, "you think what works with boys here will work with men in boarding school like Chi. It's too perfectly quaint the way you have such a swelled head about everything you do. I certainly would laugh to see you try your marvelous brain system on a passionate man like Chi."

As a matter of fact, that was just what I was planning to do. I thought it would be sort of nice to have Chi take me to the Paint and Powder. I was sure of a drag from Davy, of course, but I just happened to feel like I needed a change of air.

I was burrowing around in the umbrella stand for my skates. "Would you?" I said, my voice sounding kind of hollow on account of the umbrella stand; "well, you better start then."

"I suppose you think you can get a bid out of him for Paint and Powder?" Lysbeth asked sweetly, and before I thought I bit.

"I wouldn't be surprised," I said.

"I would," Lysbeth gloated, " 'cause he asked me last night."

Well, for a minute I kept my head in the umbrella stand and I felt as though I didn't want to ever come up, and then I realized that I must have

8

been mistaken about Chi. He couldn't be so much if he'd fallen for anything as crude as Lysbeth.

It was beginning to snow as we started down the hill — just a lazy kind of snow that whirls around and sticks to your eyelashes and the fuzz on your beret. We met Davy in his model-T coming to look for us.

"Say," he said, spraying snow all over everybody, "say, where did you falsefaces get lost to? The bunch is just about getting ready to give up and go home."

"We're coming," Pauline said, stumbling over some ruts; "why is everybody around here always in such a terrible hurry? My lunch is just turning over and over inside of me."

"You ate all that green," I reminded her, with a slight shudder. "Listen, Davy, did you save right wing for me?"

"I'm always goal," Julie said rather pitifully. "I wish to goodness I could get a chance to be something else once in a while. I just about freeze from the waist down. A person can hardly feel themselves walking home when they play goal."

"Did you, Davy?" I said, not particularly hearing Julie. It was kinder that way. Nobody has ever told Julie about the facts of life. A person simply doesn't have them in a middy and bloomers and a tippet.

9

"Mary and Chi chose up and you're on Chi's side, so you'll have to ask him," Davy said glumly. All the girls had been falling for Chi since he came home for the holidays and I could see that Davy was afraid he was going to lose me.

"I wouldn't be seen dead on Chi's side," I said, to reassure him. "See if you can't fix it for me, Davy. You know you need me at right wing."

"My goodness, listen to the girl athlete," Lysbeth said with a languid laugh, from where she had been staring pensively into the setting sun if there had been one. "I couldn't dream of ever being good enough to play with men. Why, I'm just dead now." She drooped limply over the car door and gazed up at Davy. "Do you suppose you could find a corner just to ride me a little ways? I guess I'm not such a regular husk as Maud," she said, in that fading voice that is a little like a mating call with Lysbeth.

Well, if anybody can think of any less attractive picture than me being a regular husk, I would just love to hear it. Davy and I exchanged a look of complete understanding.

"Leap in, blonde," he said to Lysbeth, "before I gag."

When we got to the pond, everybody was yelling around and telling everybody else what to do, in case somebody had never played hockey before, which everybody had. I was sitting on Bill Brandt's wind-breaker, putting on my skates, when Chi came weaving toward me, acting like a big moment coming into my life. You could pick him out from the others, he being the one that wore a nifty golf suit and a sweater with a letter on it for being on some team. We all generally wear our dimmest clothes for playing hockey because it's apt to get rough.

"Hello, Maudie," he said, banking his feet with a ruthless, scraping sound. "You're on my side. Everybody's waiting."

I seemed to get a knot in my shoe lace.

"I was just thinking," I said, hard at work, "that if you go around chewing up the ice like that, this pond will be mush before we start."

He laughed smugly and sat down on the bank with the air of a man whom women adore.

"Is that so?" he said, leaning on his elbow and leering up at me. "Say, what do you do, pal: run things around here?"

"It's funny," I said, "but nobody seems to have to run things around here. Everybody seems to just naturally know things like not digging holes in the ice with the points of their skates the way you're doing." I pensively tied my shoe.

"Is that so?" Chi said all over again, in what was meant to be a tone of sarcasm. "Ha! Ha! Come

11

on, pal, get going — Hi, beautiful!" And he skated over to where Lysbeth was just getting out of Davy's car, leaving me looking at the scenery and feeling like a wet shoe that nobody wants to wear. All my life I have wondered what an unmarried mother feels like, nobody having ever been able to quite tear themselves away from me in the past; well, here was this twerp bossing me around one minute and dumping me off the next like so much old clothes. It was a pretty grim experience. As I hunted around for where I had left my hockey stick, I quietly wished he would go drop dead somewhere.

But he didn't and in the end I had to play on his side. I was at left wing with him playing center and mentally making all the goals — you could tell by his dreamy smile. Lysbeth was sitting on the bank, where she had Davy putting on her skates and Bob Lindsay lending her his wind-breaker and Chi setting her watch, she having decided to be referee, in spite of the fact that generally when something happens we all just yell.

"Listen, everybody," Chi said, skating back to center. "Hey, listen, everybody! I'll tell you how we play at school. The wings pass back to the center instead of — Hey! Listen! Up at school the center does all the actual — Hey!"

"I simply can't understand it," I said, hitting a

dead leaf with my stick. "I should think they'd simply hang on your words."

Chi gave me a menacing look.

"I suppose you think you're pretty cute stuff, don't you, pal?" he said. "I should think this bunch would be glad to find out the way hockey is really played in a big place like St. Luke's instead of ganging around like they're doing."

"I've never noticed," I said, skating idly around in a circle, "that anybody ever got much joy out of being told how to do something they already know how to do."

Just then Davy skated over to center on the other team. "Hello, spook," he said, grinning over at me; "don't get vicious with that club."

"Maudie seems to own this ice," Chi said rather sourly, "She thinks she's quite the hockey player."

"Oke," said Davy enthusiastically, "she's a ding-er, what I mean. Just stick around. Come on, gang. Snap to."

The first period was pretty mournful. We would all mill around excitedly, waiting for a pass which nobody ever got because Chi would carry the puck himself all the way up center, getting us all out of position trying to decide where to be next — and end up by shooting into Davy; after which he would tear into everybody because we weren't

13

massed behind him like the gallant six hundred, ready to stop Davy with our lifeless forms.

"This may be a sort of human sacrifice," I remarked pleasantly to Chi, "but it isn't hockey."

"I'll say!" said Chi, missing the point. "All this crowd does is to get in the way and gum up the other fellow's try. Up at St. Lukes — "

"If I were you," I said tiredly, "I'd tie St. Luke's outside somewhere. Really!"

Chi came over and glared down at me. He really is quite impressively tall, with black hair and all the way across black eyebrows, just ideal for glaring.

"I'm getting pretty well sick of you," he said. "You crack wise any more and I'll fix you where you'll remember it. How'd you like to be spanked with this hockey stick right here in about two minutes? I'll tell you what I think of you — "

"Don't," I begged, gazing up at his scowl, "I bruise so easily."

"Hey!" Davy shouted. "Hey, call off the dogs, you two! Take out your peeve on us, why don't you? Hey, play hockey!"

I have never been much on the brawny kind of athletics, but I have a kind of a natural gift for skating, and not meaning to praise myself, nobody is on to Davy like I am. You can't shoot into Davy; you've got to rush him, and with the score 6–0 favor them, and Chi still hogging the puck, I began to realize that something drastic would have to be done. It was snowing pretty hard by then and the scenery was getting quite fuzzy.

It's funny how it happened. One minute I was edging out of right wing into the center, sort of dangling my stick, and the next thing you knew my stick had seemed to have wandered in among Chi's feet and there was a thud and a creak, as Chi's stomach hit the ice while both Chi and the ice groaned, and there I was playing the puck up right alley as though nothing had happened. It was all so quick that Chi didn't seem to know what up-dumped him and nobody else had noticed except me, and I naturally wasn't telling. Anyway, I didn't have a chance, because there was Davy big as life, trying to hook the puck. If I hadn't been used to Davy, I mightn't have made the goal.

Lysbeth was crooning over Chi as we skated back, and brushing him off, and everybody else was churning around, acting worried.

"Gosh, Chi, didn't you hurt yourself!" Pauline was twittering. "Gosh! I guess there was a sort of a hole in the ice. Anyhow, it's snowing too hard to go on, isn't it, Davy? Gosh, how can we see the puck?"

Chi didn't seem to notice them. He came over to where I was sweeping the puck up and down.

"Did you trip me?" he said, looking down at me. The snow really was getting thick and the spirit of play was definitely fading out.

"Hasn't anyone got a cigarette, if only for warmth?" Lysbeth asked everybody in general. "Honestly, I'm so cold and stiff I'll break if somebody doesn't take me home pretty soon."

"Musta forgot your pulse-warmers," Bob Lindsay said, "little hothouse flower."

"Did you trip me?" Chi said, still looking down at me.

"I just adore snow," Pauline said dreamily, until Bill Brandt pushed her from behind. "Get out, thug. If I fell down I'd split this skirt."

"It's all right to go dashing around getting health and all," Lysbeth said, sitting down on the bank and waving her eyes around, "but it's for the heart hours I am. Isn't anybody else cold?" It really was snowing hard by then.

Davy picked up a load of hockey sticks and stuffed the puck into his pocket.

"Pile in, bundle of sex," he said to Lysbeth, "and sit light. The spring's bust on your side."

Everybody was shaking snow off of their windbreakers and climbing into cars with their skates on. I started for the bank, but Chi held my arm till I about sat down.

"What did you trip me up for?" he said. I pulled at my arm.

"Well," I said, "it seemed like a good idea at the time."

"Oh, did it?" he said.

"Yes," I said, "that's my arm. Whatever you're doing, stop it."

To my surprise, he laughed and sort of hugged my arm while coasting me over to the bank. I found my shoes and got into his car, it being the only one left and I having to get home some way. He stepped over the door and pulled things and kicked things in the usual way to get us started.

"Where to?" he said, looking at me with that same laugh, only silent.

"Home," I said, trying to unwind my feet from each other.

"Oh, no," said Chi. "Oh, no, no. What eating joint, I meant. You don't suppose I want the first girl I ever fell for running out on me, do you? Fell for — did you get that, Maudie? Fell for."

"Yes, I got it," I said coldly. "I was terribly entertained. I practically choked."

"Don't be so mean," Chi said. "Think of my feelings. What do you think I am, anyway?"

"I wouldn't know at all," I said, trying to keep my teeth from banging together as we went over bumps. "You seem to go over pretty big around here, but really I personally never gave you a second thought."

Chi put on the brakes and skidded. Unexpectedly I slid over practically into his lap. He reached around me with his arm in that dogged way men have which means, "Look out, I'm getting mushy."

"What's wrong with me, pal?" he said, gently bumping my ear with the side of his head. "What's wrong with me?"

A slight shudder swept over me.

"Everything," I said, looking coldly at his handsome face. "There are some things in life that sort of gripe a person, and you're getting to be one of them. I've been riding around with quite a few boys, but I never had one sit and mash my ear and think that was charm. I like a person to have some depths." I wiggled away from him and leaned my elbow on the door and looked at the snow.

Chi laughed that laugh that was getting to be horrible.

"Come on, be a sweet Maudie," he said, leaning over toward me. "Do you want me to get an inferiority complex?"

I looked helpless.

"Can any one imagine a man with an inferiority complex?" I said, gazing around. "Well, hardly."

"So you're going to stand me up for a hot sock like Davy," he said, "Good clean American youth."

18

Well, there was no use my even mentioning the bond that lay between me and Davy. I just smiled.

"Men are always convenient to have around," I simply said, airily.

Well, one minute I was looking at the scenery and thinking pleasant thoughts about Davy and all, and the next thing I knew Chi had stalled the engine and was kissing me. It pretty nearly threw me into a swoon, but being the kind that always believes in meeting life's crisises, and being pretty well crowded over in my corner, I simply opened the door and slid quietly out, while Chi fell unexpectedly on his jaw.

"I just wish you could see how silly you look," I said, and waving my hand, I started down the road. It was a dramatic moment, but I knew in my heart that it couldn't last, because my shoes were still in the car and my skates were killing my feet. As I came to the bend where the pond road comes out on Montgomery Avenue, it came to me that whereas blessed are the pure in heart, it doesn't get them anywhere and it is the meek that inherit the earth. I leaned up against the tree and looked meekly back. Chi had finally started the car and was bumping toward me in a depressed way.

"I'm a mutt, Maudie," he said, kicking open the door. "Come on, get in, won't you, and let's go feed somewhere? I'm just a mutt, nothing but a mutt."

"Oh, no, you're not," I said kindly, "you're a very sweet boy, even if you do seem just a little young. You can't help it," I went on, encouragingly. "Anyway, I may have just a little different kind of standard; I mean, all the girls are just ga-ga over you, and Lysbeth, for instance, thinks you are a kind of an answer to her heart's cry, but you seem just a little obvious to me. But goodness, it don't matter. I'm only one person."

"But heck," Chi said, banging the horn so suddenly that people that happened to be crossing the street leaped and shot sour looks at us, "heck, you don't understand. A man has to act up to please the girls and give them what they want. It don't give me any big time muzzling some girl. I'm naturally sort of introspective with lots of thoughts, but one of these canary craniums wouldn't get much out of that. A man has to please them."

"I think it's wonderful to be so thoughtful of other people's happiness," I said, dragging on one shoe. Chi looked at me suspiciously.

"Was that a dirty dig?" he said. I sat up, rather red in the face, I feared.

"Not at all," I said. "It was just what you said. Wasn't it?"

Chi looked terribly dazed.

"Listen, Chi," I said, settling back, "why don't you just forget about me? Everybody thinks you're divine and Lysbeth adores you, and just because I happen to have been through a little more than they have — I mean, what with a few unhappy love affairs and all — well, why should you go around wasting your youth even trying to understand me? Keep your illusions, Chi," I said, staring out at some ruts. "Life is a pretty terrible thing when they're gone."

"Gosh, Maudie," Chi said, driving solemnly over the railroad bridge, "you don't mean actual love affairs? Where would you find anybody around here to fall in love with?"

"With you away it was pretty hard," I said innocently and then I became grave. "I don't go around looking for people to fall in love with, big man. Men just simply come into my life, and there I am, wondering what it's all about."

"And yet," Chi argued, "when I try to come into your life, you leave me flat. Seriously, I mean, Maudie."

"You didn't come in," I reminded him. "You broke in. A person likes a person to have some inhibitions."

"Not these other girls," Chi said.

"I thought," I said, smiling up at him, "we were talking about me."

21

Chi's expression became helplessly adoring.

"I meant — what I meant was that you aren't like these other girls. There's a kind of a mystery about you."

I thought casually in my mind about how he upset on the ice, and how he fell off me and banged his jaw in the car; and I could see how that must have seemed awfully mysterious to a perfect lover type like Chi.

"That isn't mystery," I said. "That's the instinct of self-preservation. I hate having men mush all over me."

"But gosh," Chi said, "how's a man ever going to make love to you — well, your husband, for instance? I mean, what other way is there?"

"Well," I said, "I have always believed that a person's soul was a pretty real thing."

"Yeah," said Chi, "but I'd just like to see it get real pash about any little thing. You've got to feel things, Maudie."

I gazed up at the sky as we bumped into the curb in front of the drug store and stopped. It was practically dark and the snow was piling up on our laps.

"Do you suppose," I said, "that I haven't been awakened?"

"Maudie," he began eagerly, sliding his arm behind me —

22

"Because," I went on firmly, putting his arm back where it belonged, "maybe that's the secret of my success."

I was sitting gazing dreamily into the fire and Chi had at last gone home to dinner, when Lysbeth came in, twirling her beret on her finger.

"Hello, darling," she said, flopping into a chair. "Honestly, I'm a wreck!"

"What wrecked you?" I asked pleasantly, still gazing into the fire. Lysbeth rolled her eyes and smiled smugly while roughing up her back hair.

"It was simply divine," she said. "Honestly, Davy is too cute! All he needs is to be shown things. I'm doing you a real favor, Maudie."

"That's awfully sweet of you," I said. Lysbeth waited eagerly for me to burst with curiosity, but I'm not the bursting type.

"I mean," Lysbeth went on, with the quiet pleasure of a person twisting the knife in the wound, "that by next Friday I'll have him all set to give you a time at the Paint and Powder. He's learning fast. Honestly, I can't wait to tell Chi. He will simply die of jealousy."

Well, I looked at Lysbeth and it suddenly came over me that Lysbeth didn't really know anything at all about men or she wouldn't go around practically giving herself to everybody. I smiled kindly.

23

"You're so wonderful, Lysbeth," I said, "but don't get your hopes up about Chi's dying."

"What do you mean, don't get my hopes up?" Lysbeth said with a mean look. "Chi's taking *me* to Paint and Powder, don't forget."

"I won't," I said sweetly, "but it just happens he's asked *me* up for the hockey game and the Sixth Form Dance — up at St. Luke's, you know. It lasts a whole week-end. Chi says it's the biggest event of the year," I went on, roughing up my back hair too, "and so I guess I will have to fit it in somehow." And I just thought quietly to myself about how it pays to have morals, because the less you give a man the more you get out of him.

II

THE LINE'S BUSY

WELL, life seems to be all extremes, like the people you see that are too short or too tall or too fat or too thin. And that's a deeper remark than you might imagine because it doesn't only apply to the way people look. Take Lysbeth, for instance, who knew too much about sex for her own good, and then at Christmas time along came my cousin Joy, who didn't know enough. This was obvious before the Cinderella Dance we were at had hardly got going.

"Don't laugh if it hurts," Bill Brandt was saying to me reproachfully, and I realized with horror that I had missed the point of some joke he was telling,

25

and you know what that does to your stock with a boy; but how could I listen to his rattle with Davy's agonized eyes searing my very soul? Davy was at least the sixth boy I'd gotten to dance with Joy and the drizzle hadn't had one cut back. Davy was doing all he could; I could see that. Every time he and Joy came to the stag line, he danced along slow right up close and started talking and laughing a lot, as though he was having a wonderful time, but it was no sale. And now he was just dragging her around as dumb as a mummy and looking at me like a drowning man going down for the third time. I realized that something must be done — and quickly too.

Luckily at that point Davy started putting on his act in front of the stag line again. "Bill," I said, "see that foreign matter in our midst that Davy's giving a whirl?"

"Yeah," Bill said, without much enthusiasm. He was still feeling a little huffy on account of my missing his joke.

"Well, she's my cousin, Joy Saunders from Baltimore, and you'll have an eternal drag with me if you'll dance with her. You'll be cut in on right away." I did my best to make my voice sound convincing, and just then the music stopped and I started to pull him along over to them.

"Hey, wait a minute," Bill said, in the tones

of a person looking for a catch somewhere, and pulling back; "promise you won't let me get stuck? Promise?"

"Oh, all right," I said, very much on my dignity with my nose in the air, "if that's the way you feel about it. I only suggested it because Joy told me she wanted to meet you because she knows somebody that knows you and thinks you're the answer to a maiden's prayer — though why, I can't imagine."

"Now who the dickens do I know in Baltimore?" Bill said, with a pleased expression.

"Well," I said, "as long as you don't deign to dance with Joy you'll never find out — and some poor girl will die of a broken heart."

"Aw, climb down off your high horse, Maudie," Bill said pleadingly; "I was only fooling. I'd do anything for you. You know that, Maudie."

"All right, Sir Galahad," I said, appearing to relent, and I took him over and introduced him to Joy. Then the music started and I started dancing with Davy. I saw Bill talking very earnestly to Joy and laughing sort of coyly and I knew he was trying to find out which maiden's prayer he was the answer to. Joy just looked dumb and shook her head and I felt absolutely sick with rage. Here I'd fixed it so she could get a rush out of Bill all evening and she didn't play up. And she was to

27

stay until after Christmas. I felt old before my time. How was I ever going to swing a girl like that?

Davy was beefing about the way I'd let him get stuck.

"My goodness," I said, "you don't think she enjoyed it any more than you did, do you? And you were only stuck with her ten minutes, anyway."

"Ten minutes?" Davy said. "It seemed like hours."

"You might at least be polite enough to remember that after all she's my cousin," I said witheringly. But Davy's not the type that you can wither.

"That's not your fault, is it?" he said reasonably. Maybe it wasn't, but just the same I was going to have Joy on my neck like the Old Man of the Sea for the next week, and it was up to me to see that she had some kind of a time. After all, blood is thicker than water, even if it is only a cousin's; and besides, I knew if I didn't look out for Joy, Mother wouldn't let me have those new dinner pajamas I was counting on, like she threatened not to when I tried to keep her from inviting the droop in the first place.

Bill came plowing past us, bumping Joy into people in that careless way boys have with girls they're stuck with that they wouldn't mind seeing

28

break a leg or something, and I will never forget the *et tu Brute* look he gave me. This was turning out to be a large evening for me, all right.

"Davy," I hissed, "bump into Joy and muss up her hair with your elbow, will you?"

"With pleasure," said Davy. He did it almost too well. For a minute I thought he'd knocked the poor girl out. While he was apologizing in a positively courtly manner, I linked arms with Joy, who was still groggy, and suggested we repair the ravages in the dressing room. Perhaps my crop of ragged ends could stand a little fixing too. "Meet us at the door in ten minutes," I said to Davy, "with another boy," and I gave him a look that spoke volumes. Bill had melted artfully into the crowd the minute Joy let go of him, but my friendship with him was purely platonic, whereas between Davy and I things were on a different plane entirely, so I knew I could count on him being there, even if he had to beat up the other boy to get him.

There were the usual sad sights in the dressing room — several short-suited girls talking and laughing and trying very hard to seem busy fixing their hair or something, in the fond hope that nobody would guess they'd been hopelessly stuck and were doomed to die on the vine, barring miracles, for the rest of the evening. Julie Purviance was there too, as usual, calmly reading a book.

29

Julie is one of those types that besides having absolutely no sex appeal, has what the teachers at school call a fine mind. Why is it the people with fine minds are all always so dumb about the things that really count? As I looked at Joy taking down her hair that Davy had completely wrecked, I'd have bet a month's candy she was an honor student.

"Listen, you goop," I hissed low and intense, "what did you say to Bill?"

Joy turned and gave me a delightfully vague expression, her mouth full of hairpins. "Why, he seemed to think I had a message or something for him from somebody in Baltimore, which of course I hadn't."

"You — you didn't tell him that?" I groaned.

"Of course I did, but he wouldn't believe me though, for the longest time. Aren't boys silly?"

I happened to see my agonized expression in the mirror just then and took a good look at it, so I'd know how to make it again if ever I wanted to.

"He kept asking and asking," Joy babbled on, "until I got annoyed beyond words and told him not to be inane."

I mentally tore my hair, though not actually, as it had far too perfect an air of careless abandon to take any chances with it. "Dumb," I muttered, "just absolutely, hopelessly, terribly dumb."

"He is, isn't he," Joy said brightly, missing the point that I was talking about her.

"Don't you realize that you could have had Bill rushing you all evening, caboose?" I said with heat.

"How do you mean?" Joy asked, missing the insult of "caboose," as she really is very slow in catching on.

Well, I've never pictured myself as giving advice to the lovelorn like Dorothy Dix but I must admit I seem to have a way with men. So I explained to her how they're all terribly conceited and curious and if they think you've heard somebody say something about them they'll do anything to find out what.

Taking a peek out the door, I saw that Davy had lassoed Chi but was having difficulty in holding him and I knew that there was no time to lose going into details with Joy. "Listen," I said, "you do what I say and I'll explain later. When Davy introduces Chi to you say, 'Imagine seeing you here; I've heard so many terrible things about you!' Chi's the type that thinks he's irresistible and he'll keep on coming back all evening to find out what you've heard, only don't tell him, which won't be hard not to, as you really haven't heard anything about him not to tell, see? I'll tell everybody that cuts in on me that my pretty cousin from Baltimore has heard things about them and they'll all give you a rush to find out what. Treat 'em rough and tell 'em nothing, and everything's going to be slick," I said reassuringly, while pushing Joy, who looked all aghast and agog, toward the door. "Just look wise and if you can't think of anything to say, say 'I'm too smart for that.' I use it by the hour."

Well, Joy got off the line to Chi about having heard so many terrible things about him in a sort of a scared tone of voice, but it went over big just the same. You could see Chi getting interested right away and as he whirled her off, after whispering something in her ear, I heard her say, "I'm too smart for that." I began to feel more cheerful, as it looked like Joy — even if she didn't know anything — wasn't too dumb to learn; and besides, she could be made quite attractive in an exotic way if you overlooked the freckles that people with her kind of orange-colored hair always seem to have. Besides being almost an ash blonde with a milky white complexion that knows how to wear clothes, I am of a naturally kindly disposition and I felt very pleased as I thought of how grateful she was going to be for the happiness I was bringing into her life. Gratitude! Ha, ha. I still laugh, though no longer bitterly.

Bill cut in on me and Davy, and I got him believing again that Joy had actually heard something about him and was holding out on him because it was too terrible to repeat. I saw him cut in on her as soon as he left me, and then I gave the same line to everyone that danced with me. I told the conceited ones that Joy had heard something terrible about them and the unattractive or shy ones that she had heard somebody rave about them, and pretty soon Joy was getting a wonderful rush. I was having a lot of fun seeing Joy have such a good time and knowing she owed it all to me, and I began to wonder why one girl didn't lend a helping hand to a weak sister oftener. Alas, I was to learn.

Davy hadn't minded bringing Joy along with me to the party, but I knew he wouldn't get any big boot out of a chummy little threesome on the way home, and I didn't exactly relish the idea either, so I got Joy off in a corner, along toward the end of the evening, and tactfully told her that I thought it would be swell if she went home with Chi or anybody else besides me and Davy.

"But I just can't ask Chi to take me home, Maudie," Joy protested.

"Of course not," I said patiently. "You've got to be subtle about it. Just ask him to lend you a nickel."

"What for?" the dumb girl asked.

"That's just what Chi will say," I said, "and then you say you think you'll be a crowd going home with Davy and me and you want to 'phone the taxi place to come around and pick you up."

"Oh, I see, now," Joy said, with a gleam of almost human intelligence in her green eyes. "Then Chi will ask if he can't take me home."

"Check," I said, "and if he don't, just keep his nickel and borrow one from somebody else."

When I got home, Joy was already there, crying with rage on my bed. "There's no excuse for that man," she gnashed.

"There, there," I soothed, "tell mother all about it. And please stop crying on my pillow. Remember I have to sleep on it."

Well, it seemed that Chi had made a pass at Joy when they got to the door and she hadn't wanted to hurt his feelings or seem to be a prig by acting offended, so she tried to appeal to his better self. That was a big mistake, as Joy soon found out, because men haven't any better self when it comes to wanting their way with a girl.

Chi told her she was absolutely right to lay off this petting and he respected her for it. But he tried to tell her that a girl who won't show a man she likes him a little by letting him kiss her good night, she simply isn't on the team, that's all. "Just a friendly little kiss — " and with that he pulled her to him by the hand she had trustingly stuck out for a moral good night and grabbing her by the scruff of the neck with his other hand, he kissed her till she almost suffocated.

Joy started sobbing on my pillow again when she reached this point. "I think boys are disgusting," she said. "They're nothing but animals. I hate them — all of them."

Well, I was a little puzzled about Joy's being so violent, because after all, even if you don't like it, being kissed by force is a kind of a compliment to one's charm, and I suspected that Joy hadn't told all. It turned out I was right, though it took quite a while to finally worm the truth out of her. When Chi finally had to let her go and come up for air, she slapped him and called him an egg.

"Well, who laid you?" he asked coldly and turned on his heel and left. That's what really griped her. It made me pretty mad too and I resolved right there that for the honor of my sex I was going to develop Joy's technique so she could get anybody she wanted, Chi included.

There was plenty to work on, as she had a neat little figure and unusual face and hair and green eyes and a good complexion, except for the freckles. I could see all she needed was the right clothes and make-up and a little fixing to be exotic and alluring instead of just plain dumb-looking, like she didn't know what it was all about. I was glad she didn't like the boys to pet or even neck her, as it is fatal to get a rep for being easy. You can't be a real heart-breaker without ideals. I belong to an anti-petting and necking club myself that a bunch of us girls have organized that anybody gets thrown out of it on their ear if they even let anybody kiss her — even the boy they are most in love with. This is not always easy to tell anyhow, as love is such a fickle thing. I have been truly in love with four boys at one time.

"There's lots of ways to handle boys when they start to get mushy," I said, dumping the things out of my beaded bag, "only a person has to be subtle. For instance, I often suck a couple of licorice drops on the way home from a dance and then if a boy starts anything, all you have to do is to gently blow a licorice breath in his face. It's a wonderful protection. Chewing gum is a good idea too. You just crack it at the psychological moment."

"You make it sound easy," Joy said in skeptical tones, though drying her tears and getting up off my clean nightie, "just like those soap ads that say all you've got to do to be popular is to wash your face and be natural. I tried it, but when I walked down the hall naturally at school, the boys didn't all yell 'Look! she's natural,' and plunge after me."

"Of course not," I said, "a clean face helps, I suppose, but it don't get you anywhere to be natural, unless you're naturally charming. The important thing is to *seem* natural, but you can't expect the men that write those ads to know that. They see a girl getting away big and being the life of the party, and they think she's acting natural, when maybe she's all frozen up inside and not acting natural at all."

"But when I freeze up that way, like when I've just met a very popular boy, I can't think of anything to say at all. And pretty soon the boy begins to act as if they were under a strain."

"You don't have to say anything," I said in muffled tones, while wriggling out of my dress, "if you just convey the impression that you're not talking because you can't be bothered instead of because you don't know how. Like Greta Garbo, who gets credit for being a mystery woman when probably it's simply that she's too dumb to think of anything to say."

"Well, I always feel as though it would be easier to talk and I want to say something," Joy said plaintively, "but I get feeling all hollow inside and can't think of a thing. Mother says just flatter the boys and you'll be popular but that doesn't work either. I tried telling Davy how well he danced and he got all embarrassed and said, 'What do I do now, grow wings?' and then he stepped on my foot."

37

"Your mother was a girl a long time ago," I said gently. "These boys to-day are sophisticated; you've got to be subtle with them."

"How do you mean?" Joy said eagerly, peeling off her stockings.

"Well, for instance, suppose you're dancing with a skinny guy, ask him if he rows on the crew. Then when he asks you all pleased why you thought he rowed on the crew, say 'because you have such broad shoulders.' And you sort of nestle up against him. That's being subtle. Or if you're introduced to a great big clumsy oaf that can't get out of his own way, ask him if he sings in the glee club."

"Whatever for?"

"He'll want to know what gave you the idea, and then you give him a melting look and tell him you thought he must sing, he has such a pleasant speaking voice. See if you can reach this pin down my back, Joy. I nearly sprained my shoulder putting it in.

"Then when you know a boy a little better, you can tell him what you think his character is, or that you've had a dream about him. They love that. And if a boy is the shy type sometimes it helps to be very cordial to him, like when he cuts in give his hand a little squeeze and say, 'I saw you in the stag line and just hoped you'd dance with me.' Or tell somebody else that you're simply pash about that boy and the person you tell it to is sure to repeat it to him, because boys are much worse gossips than girls. The conceited boys that think they're wonderful you get more interested if you tell them you think they're terrible. It never fails to get a rise out of them and they immediately give you a big rush to show you you're all wrong."

Joy was drinking it all in, I could see that, and speaking of flattery, I guess I was a little flattered by having such an avid audience myself or else I would have had too much sense to give away my entire line to her like I did.

"But my main trouble is I don't know how to get started with a boy," Joy began again. "I can't ever think what to say first, before you know what kind of a boy he is or what he's interested in or anything."

"I use the sophistication test on a new boy sometimes," I said.

"What's that?"

"Ask a boy 'What experience have you had?' and then you can rate him by the way he answers. If he gets all flustered and blushes and doesn't know what to say, he's unsophisticated and needs one kind of a line; and if he comes back with a wisecrack like 'You should see my references', he's the coldly intellectual type that you can kid along in perfect safety; but watch out for the impetuous ones that say, 'How about my giving you a demonstration?' "

"Gosh," Joy said, taking hairpins out of her hair in an awed way.

"Sure," I said. "Then boys love to have you ask favors of them; it makes them feel so sort of masculine and protective. I'll tell a boy there's somebody here I just can't bear to dance with and will he cut in on me if he sees me make a sign like making my hand on the boy's back into a fist or something. He'll keep cutting back and back even without the sign, just to be sure he's protecting me, and he'll want to know what I've got against the boy and all and that gives us plenty to talk about if I use my imagination a little."

"But suppose it isn't true?" Joy said.

"It usually isn't," I said.

"Another way to have a rush is to get your feelings hurt. Pretend that the boy has said something about you that has been repeated to you and you are just terribly, terribly hurt. He'll keep coming back to find out what it was and after a while you can make up something and tell him, and when he denies it say you were told it on good authority, and then he'll rush you the rest of the evening to find out who it was and finally you can say you forgive him anyhow and have a sweet reconciliation."

It was amazing how much I seemed to know. Even after we were in bed with the light out I kept remembering things, like when a boy cuts in the first time in an evening and you say, 'Well, I suppose this is your duty dance, isn't it?' Then he has to come at least twice to prove it wasn't. Or like giving him something of yours to keep, as for instance a vanity box, or just as he's being cut out start to say something interesting that he'll want to cut back to hear the end of.

"But what if they want to sit out?" Joy said, propping herself up on her elbow. "I get scared every time the music stops."

I yawned. It really was awfully late.

"Well," I said, "it's a good idea to start telling him your dreams and ambitions, like being a nurse so you can take care of people and ease their suffering, or how wonderful to be the inspiration of some man — and then you're on to marriage and the boy is sure to have his own ideas on that topic and you're set for the evening. And then, of course, you ought to seem to be interested in a boy's thoughts and things like his career, and whether his team won last year, and all."

Well, Joy sopped up everything I told her like a sponge and she was so pathetically grateful that for the next couple of days I felt like a whole troop of girl scouts and the Good Samaritan rolled into

41

one, as I helped her to get popular. Besides working on her line, I showed her what to do with her
hair and how to make up. I taught her everything
I knew myself and that wasn't a little bit. And for
the Barringer's Christmas Eve dance at the Cricket
Club, I got an orchid-colored dress of Mother's
that we fixed over and with that and long green
earrings and green slippers and orange curls standing up all over her head like flames, you wouldn't
have guessed in a million years that Joy was the
same person that I had to get people to dance with
as a personal favor to me the week before. She was
a riot. She panicked the party. What little time
she spent on the floor she didn't get to dance more
than two steps with a boy and there was a line fol-
lowing her around, fighting to cut in. I was practically a wallflower by comparison, and every boy
that did dance with me couldn't talk about anything else but Joy, so although it was very satisfying to realize that I had done so much for her, I
began to wonder if maybe I'd done a little too
much.

Bob Lindsay was carrying her compact for her
and Henry Rollins her purse. Bill Brandt was protecting her from somebody she'd confided in him
she couldn't bear to dance with — he hadn't found
out who it was yet — and Freddie Kemp almost
wept on my hair because she told him that he had

hurt her terribly — something he'd said that had been repeated to her, she wouldn't tell him what. Bing Mason told me how she'd sat out with him and read his character and told him he ought to be a doctor because he was so sympathetic — Bing plays football and is boxing champion of his school. Somebody else told me all about her sweet soul and how she wanted to study to be a nurse so she could ease people's suffering. Davy and Chi pretended to be foaming with rage because of the way she'd been insulting them, but I could see that really they were intrigued. For the first time in my life I was glad when the orchestra started to play "Good Night Ladies." I was dancing with Chi at the time and he clapped loudly for an encore. I wasn't particularly flattered, though, because I suspected he was hoping somebody'd cut in on us he could have one last whirl with Joy, at whom he was shamelessly making eyes.

"Hi, Maudie," Joy yelled over the heads of the boys who completely surrounded her, "who's your friend in the high-button shoes?" Everybody laughed and Chi grinned sheepishly and then the music started. Davy cut Chi out and sure enough Chi made a bee line for Joy. Davy had a sort of a guilty expression, as he hadn't been near me in at least an hour.

"Well, Davy," I said lightly and yet with a certain touch of cool dignity, "nice to see you after all these years."

"I had to take that red-headed job outside and tell her a few things," Davy said. "That's where I been. She's got the wrong idea about me entirely."

"Really?" I said.

"Aw, Maudie," Davy crooned softly, while clasping me closer, "you're not jealous, are you? Aw — "

"I can get a bird's-eye view of myself being jealous about you," I said with hauteur, pulling away from his shirt front. "I can just see myself wringing my hands in grief and maybe even pulling out a little piece of my hair where it won't show. I — "

Suddenly I realized that the music had stopped and I was going right on yelling at the top of my lungs in the silence, the way you will sometimes. I shut up, very much embarrassed and in a most unpleasant state of mind.

"Little girls shouldn't try to be sarcastic," Davy said, like a condescending pat on the head. "People won't like you and dogs will bark at you."

"I'm not *trying* to be anything," I said, closer to tears than I have been in years. "I'm being myself."

"Well, be some one else then," Davy said calmly.

Oh, the bitter tragedy of that moment when I knew that I had lost my power over him!

Life goes on, however, and it's laugh, clown, laugh, when your heart is breaking or even already broken inside. At that very moment, as I stood in the midst of the ruins of my life, Chi came up, with Joy drooping on his arm.

"Maudie," Joy said, "come with me into the dressing room, won't you? I'm simply a wreck."

As we stood in front of the glass, I waited for Joy to at least give me the cold comfort of a little gratitude, but she didn't — just went chirping on about how mussed her hair was, and how she'd literally danced her legs off to the hips, my dear.

"Very different from the kind of a time you had last week, isn't it?" I said to take her down a peg or two, "I guess you realize now what a potent line — "

"Oh, I don't know," Joy drawled condescendingly, and then what do you think she had the nerve to pull? "The boys are just a little slow to catch on to anything new around here."

"What?" I said, not being able to believe I heard right.

"Oh, I guess it always takes a few days for people to get to know you," she said airily. "They're awfully sweet now, though; I seem to kind of appeal to them." She put on the rouge I had bought her with my own money and laughed smugly. "Wasn't it cute of you to be so worried about me last week?" And she waltzed out, not even waiting for me.

Well, I was so mad that my teeth chattered. And the horrible part was that everybody begged Betty Barringer not to let the party stop and she persuaded her mother to have the orchestra go on another hour, and the evening got worse and worse for me. I suppose I looked like a pickle, if I looked the way I felt, and the boys were flocking around Joy.

Chi was dragging me around after Bill Brandt and Joy, so he could shout clever things at Joy over my shoulder, and I was so completely broken in spirit that I was just letting him without a struggle, when the door from the ballroom into the main part of the country club opened and three men came in. One was old Mr. Tait and one was John Harvey, a friend of my sister Sylvia's, and the other one was a tall, impressive-looking man that I had never seen before. They all sat down in the corner with cigars and ashtrays, and began pointing at us and laughing and laughing, like people at the zoo do when the monkeys do something almost human. After a while the tall man said something to John and old Mr. Tait laughed

46

in a devilish way, and John took the tall man out on the floor and introduced him to his sister, Loretta Harvey, one of our crowd, who was so overawed that she fell over his feet when they started to dance and never did get re-routed.

"Hello, sad-eye," said an unwelcome voice over my shoulder, and I saw Bob Lindsay's toothful face peering in at me; "who croaked?"

"Are you trying to break?" said Chi, with what sounded to me like a lilt in his voice.

"Sure," said Bob; "came to take the load off you. Listen, wait till I tell you what Joy got off — "

"Wait till I tell *you*," Chi bubbled. "Somebody ought to spank that girl." And he rushed off to cut in.

Well I could hardly believe it myself when I realized that I had said nothing. I just looked over at Joy and thought bitter thoughts about gratitude and blood ties and how families are supposed to stick together. And just that minute the tall man that I had never seen before cut in on Joy.

"See that big guy dancing with Joy," Bob said, pushing me around so I could drink it in, "that's Tod Robertson."

"Who's he?" I said. Bob glared at me.

"You never heard of Tod Robertson? Why, he's the big shot in polo."

"Oh," I said. Ordinarily I would have cared.

We danced on for what seemed like hours. The tall man cut back on Joy, and Bob kept babbling on about her until just as I was about to scream in his ear or bite it, an arm separated us.

"Will you introduce me to this lady, kid?" a rumbling voice said to Bob. "This can't wait for Johnny to show up."

I looked up at Tod Robertson's brownish face and square head, and noticed the way he was smiling at me just the way he had smiled at Joy. I knew in a minute that it was the time and the place for the sophistication test.

"What — " I began, and then my mind drew a blank as I realized with horror that Joy had probably used the sophistication test. And if she hadn't, how could I know what she had used? Nothing was safe.

I looked up at Tod Robertson again and he was still smiling, but his smile had changed. It was at that minute that it swept over me that the difference between me and Joy was my talent for emergencies. Here I'd been morbidly thinking all evening that there wasn't any difference, what with Joy knocking them dead all around the room and me getting to be more of a dud every few minutes. But a Leo-man like this polo hero is an absolute challenge to a person's inferiority complex to get up and fight. I looked at him, and as I hadn't

48

smiled yet (out of fright) I didn't start. I just went on looking.

"I suppose I'm a disappointment," he said, dancing in a way that made all other legs seem wooden. "Am I?"

"I don't know," I said; "I never heard of you, so I wasn't expecting anything."

He gave practically a roar of laughter.

"You win," he said. "That did sound pretty snoddy. I simply meant that I suppose you had seen us sneak in."

"Yes, I saw you," I said, giving Davy a pleasant smile as he went rubber-necking by. "Were you ever at the zoo?"

He looked down at me quickly.

"Not for years," he said. "Why?"

"I just wondered which you liked best," I said — "us or gorillas."

Davy cut in at that point, and Joy and that dumb little Ralph Preston passed, and I could hear Joy saying, "You must be on the crew." A kindly pity filled my soul.

"Say, Maudie," Davy said, rushing me off, "that's that big polo shot, Tod Robertson; didja know that?"

"Really?" I said. "Well, just swinging a stick around never got a person very far with me. How's Joy?"

Then somebody else cut in and then Tod Robertson was back again.

"Look here," he said, "I'm in wrong, I can see. Did you really mind our watching your dance? We didn't act very badly, did we?"

"No," I said, suddenly giving him my sweetest smile. "Since I last saw you, everybody has been telling me how great you are, and you have to sort of make allowances for a person that's famous."

"Good gosh," he said, "it sounds like a disease. Anyway, I'm not famous in the least," he added, looking very pleased as though neither he nor I believed him for a minute.

"Aren't you?" I said, looking at the way his ear fit into his hair. "Well, are you glad or sorry?"

Then a perfect string of people cut in and I noticed casually that Tod wasn't dancing with anybody else. As soon as he could break his way in, he cut back and ran me all the way across the room backwards, just as though they weren't playing a waltz.

"This way out," he said; "how can anybody be expected to talk in this din?" And he hustled me out the side door into the trophy room, where all the cups people win are.

"You aren't supposed to talk at a dance," I said; "it's so sort of impolite to the orchestra."

We felt our way around in the gloom, as there

weren't any lights on, and finally found a corner of a table without any cups on it to sit on. I swung my feet and looked out through a window at the twisty tips of trees brushing up against the stars, while the music floated in softly and I wondered where I had been all evening.

"Now," Tod said, "go ahead and talk. You fascinate me. Why are you so different from all these other kids — girls, I mean — that I met tonight?"

"You guess first," I said; "I can't just turn on and off like water."

"Well," he said, "they were all working so hard. You seemed effortless, if that's any way of describing it."

"I wasn't effortless," I said. "I was tongue-tied, I made a terrible mistake this week."

"How do you mean?" He looked amused.

"Well, I gave away my line. A girl might as well lose her reputation. And when you came along, I couldn't say anything because my line was here to-night, and you'd already heard it." I waved a helpless hand.

Tod was leaning forward, half-laughing.

"Are you telling me the truth?" he demanded.

"Of course I'm telling you the truth," I said. "The truth is all I've got left." I stood up, and he reached out and put his arm across my shoulders.

"Where're you going?" he said.

"Back to dance," I said, wiggling away from his embrace. "This is a dance, you know."

"Well, let's dance right out here," he said, catching me again in his arms, but I stepped out.

"No, let's don't," I said, leaning up against the table wearily; "you might try to kiss me."

"Well, for heaven's sake," he said, laughing loudly, "we do have a good opinion of ourself. Why, I have no intention of kissing you, absolutely no intention whatever."

I gave him a long dreamy look.

"Then," I said, "you aren't human."

A few hours later, Tod's car stopped at our door. The house was dark, all but a light on the stairs, and I realized for the first time how late it probably was.

"Maudie, you've got to come to the matches in the spring," Tod was saying, holding the door so that I couldn't get out.

"No," I said firmly, "I don't like to be just one of your public. I like to yell all by myself."

"But a person would starve on the few crumbs you give away, woman," said Tod, sadly opening the door. "I've never seen so much resistance in one so young."

"I've got ideals," I said. "How do you think I'd like having you point at me some day and say casu-

*"Why, I have no intention of kissing you,
absolutely no intention whatever."*

ally to your wife, "There's one of the girls I kissed."

"But Maudie — " Tod began, but I opened the front door.

"I never want to be any man's past," I said. "Good night."

As I lay in bed, thinking important thoughts, I realized happily that I had learned something new about men. There are times when no line is the best line of all.

III

SAPPY NEW YEAR

DAVY was lying on our library sofa, glumly reading a funny paper he'd fished out of the wood basket, when I came in.

"Hello," I said, throwing my beret on the piano with the air of a person that don't have to look in the mirror every time they take their hat off, "why so lemon-faced?"

"I just came around, Maudie," Davy said in a dead voice, "to see if you'd go on this New Year's Eve brawl my family's throwing for my sister Ting to-morrow night."

Davy had been broken-hearted for at least a day after Joy went home but he was now starting to take notice again and giving me the old rush, and

56

I was being big and letting bygones be bygones, because there weren't any more attractive men in sight, and who's around, after all, has an awful lot to do with who you're in love with. If Davy and I were marooned somewhere on a desert isle with nobody else there to choose from, we'd probably end up by getting married.

"I thought Ting's party was going to be all grown-ups," I said, unzipping my galoshes.

"It is," Davy said. "A bunch of graybeards, and this mob of sis's, and me. The family thought they were doing me such a big favor letting me go, I didn't have the heart to tell 'em how I felt about it. So I thought I'd ask you. It sure would be super if you could come," he ended gloomily.

Well, the idea of me actually being at the Ritz on New Year's Eve, with all the horns and bells and everybody throwing confetti and drinking champagne and everything like you read about was almost too much.

"Well, for crying in a bucket!" I said, rather annoyed with Davy for being so blah about it. "Of course I'll come. Rather divine, I think it will be."

And when I thought of going on a party with Ting, I was simply overcome. When I was a child I adored Ting — I mean, I used to lean out the school window feeling absolutely exalted just

57

watching her waiting for a trolley, and once I wrote a poem to her. Of course, I have rather outgrown that intense age since I grew up, but I still look on her with the affection a person has for things in their past, and wonder casually sometimes how she ever happened to be Davy's sister.

Davy grunted in a not very flattering way, considering I had just given him the great pleasure of accepting his invitation, but under the circumstances I let it pass.

"My goodness, Davy," I said, sitting down on his feet and thus making him move them, "I never heard anything so absolutely supreme. Aren't you sort of excited?"

"Yeah," said Davy. "Oh, yeah!"

"Then my goodness," I said, "what do you lie around acting so hit in the head for?' '

"If you had a perfectly good family," Davy said, "and then some pud tried to muscle into it, I guess you'd think you had some reason to be sunk."

"How do you mean?" I said.

"I'll bet you money Ting's engaged," he said. "Bend that one."

I stared at him aghast and then my soul filled with sad joy and understanding. "I know how you must feel, losing her," I said gently, "but think what a swell wife and mother she would make."

"Losing her, heck," said Davy. "It's what we'd

58

get back. I just wish you could see this great ache that hangs around our house all the time. I feel like I want to be sick every time I see him. 'Heigh-ho, Brother Davy.' Awrrk!" and I honestly thought Davy was going to be sick right there on the new sofa.

"Who is he?" I said, shuddering.

"Hubert Spencer," Davy said, "this guy they call Hubie. Awrrk!"

Well, of course, everybody has heard about Hubert Spencer and how every girl from Sylvia's crowd up to regular married widows think he's the P. M. — Perfect Man — and the answer to everybody's soul's yearning, which gives a pretty good idea of the souls around here. I'd heard Sylvia mushing along about his long eyelashes and his small ears until I was bored to a frenzy, but naturally I gave Ting credit for a little sense. Davy's revelation was a great shock to me.

"Davy, I think that's about the worst I ever heard," I said. "But maybe you're mistaken."

"I know what I know," Davy said darkly. "Haven't I watched 'em lollygogging by the hour? Ting would never let him get away with that stuff if she wasn't nuts about him."

"Well, now listen, Davy," I said, seeing a brighter side. "After all, if Ting likes him, he can't be so bad."

"Don't I know a sap when I see one?" Davy said. "This sap is an absolute pud, what I mean, and if you can get any joy out of watching him and Ting getting goo over each other to-morrow night — well, I'm asking you along."

I was just sitting there, thinking how depressed Davy was and how depressed I was probably going to be when I met this Hubie, when my sister Sylvia and Mother boiled in from some tea all a-twitter.

"And what have the Dillons been doing," Mother said gaily, trying to pump Davy, "keeping us all in the dark like this? What's all this we hear about Ting, the dear child?"

"Hubie's a knock-out," Sylvia said, throwing her gloves on the piano with that cold-as-charity smile of one good friend congratulating another on getting her man. "Everybody thinks he's an absolute knock-out."

"Think of a wedding in the family, Davy," Mother said, who had been thinking about it around home without much results; "wouldn't you be excited?"

Davy tried to smile, but I could see how it hurt him from the positively terrible expression underneath. "I'd rather go to his wake any day," he muttered. Mother and Sylvia simply screamed. Older people can be so shallow that a person sometimes wonders what the world would be like if there was no youth.

I was about to fling myself in when Davy said, "The family is going on a bender to-morrow night and I was asking Maud."

"To the Ritz and all," I said, knowing how Sylvia felt about my age going to the Ritz.

"Maud would be delighted to accept," Mother said, and then before I had a chance to die of joy, "Sylvia is going — Ting invited her this afternoon — and she'll keep an eye on Maudie."

Well, I just swept Sylvia with a languid smile. I could imagine how worn-out her eye was going to get, what with one thing and another.

"I had a little chat with Mrs. Lewis and Mrs. Wheeler," Mother said, after Davy had gone, "and they seemed to think that this would be a catch for Ting, if there was anything in it. Of course, I don't know the young man, so I couldn't judge."

"It's all very well to catch Hubie," said Sylvia, "but it isn't going to be so easy to hold him."

"Says she, hopefully," I put in.

"Mother, Maud honestly gets fresher every day," Sylvia went on crossly. "Anybody that knows Hubie could tell you what a fusser he is and what a heavy line he's got for every woman he meets. He's darned attractive, but believe me, you couldn't pay me to marry anybody that fickle."

"Well, if everybody knows it, why doesn't Ting?" I asked reasonably.

Sylvia eyed me pityingly.

"Ting, darling, is one of the most immature people I know, for her age — emotionally, I mean."

"Oh, I shouldn't say that, Sylvia," Mother said, picking up the evening mail. "She's a dreamy child, but she has very fine ideals."

"Yeah," Sylvia said, "one of them is she thinks that everybody is naturally good. She jumps on you if you just imply that somebody isn't perfect."

"I think that's very sweet," Mother said.

"Oh, it's sweet and all that," Sylvia said, "but my dear, look at what happens. She meets Hubie, he hands her a big line, and she falls for it, when anybody could tell her he does it to every girl he meets."

"Well, he doesn't fall in love with them all," I said, with a stubborn expression.

"You mean Ting acts as if he didn't. Somebody ought to tell her. We've all had a certain amount of experience with Hubie." Sylvia sank back into a chair with her most divorcée sigh.

"Blah," I said dispassionately. "Ting dug your cellar, and you're all mad."

Sylvia sprang up and flung herself at me.

"You make me absolutely sick!" she said. "You're the biggest dumb-bell and the silliest little poseur —"

"Girls," Mother said, "you're both too old to quarrel."

"We're not quarreling," I said pleasantly. "We just bore each other, that's all."

Well, then Sylvia began giving Mother a lot of good advice about the kind of an impression I ought to make and what I ought to wear and say and all, but mother was full of good ideas of her own.

"Dear, it was very sweet of Mrs. Dillon to include you in Ting's party," she said, turning on the reading lamp by her chair, "and I want you to try and remember that you are with older people and that it will reflect on me if you don't have good manners."

"And above everything, Mother, don't let her wear that disgusting yellow dress with no back," Sylvia said, drumming on the piano. "I don't see why you let Maudie pick out her own clothes. She's much too young to have any judgment and anyhow she always goes and gets the kind of dress I wear —"

"The kind you wear!" I exclaimed scornfully. "I'd just like to see you pry that dress down over your fanny."

"Maud," Mother said, "don't be vulgar. We'll select your most suitable dress for to-morrow night. At present, I want you to remember that Mr. and Mrs. Dillon are friends of father's and mine and I want you to behave."

Davy honked for me the next night a little before eight and I tore right out so we wouldn't be late. I was wearing my yellow dress. I just mention it in passing. When we got to the theater, not another soul in the party had come. I was never more amazed in all my life. It got to be quarter after eight and still nobody had come, and I was just about wondering if this was the right night when the curtain went up and there was a man sitting on some cellar steps singing about a jiggle-o or something, with another man just thinking on the top step. He kept trying to rest his elbows on his knees and then his knees would spread apart and he would fall through, until really Davy and I nearly died laughing. I honestly laughed till I nearly got the hiccups, and Davy was practically rolling in the aisle, when about a thousand people started squeezing past us in the dark, making us very annoyed. We kept trying to see and just then a body would go by and some elbow carrying a coat would practically sweep my hair off my head, and once some one stood on my feet for quite a few minutes.

"Please forgive, little one," said a deep sort of

I was wearing my yellow dress.

sobbing voice, climbing off my new slippers and over my knees.

"I will," I said, "but it's asking a lot of my feet."

"That's him," Davy growled in my ear. "Sap!"

I looked down the row in the dark to where he was fitting himself into his seat. He looked like the type that thinks a party is just made for them to be the life of — a sort of a cute man always laughing and saying cute things. He had fuzz on the top of his head instead of hair any more and a little bulge over the back of his collar which I'll bet he didn't know was there.

Ting looked as happy as an angel as she went past and very beautiful in a white shiny dress. Just like I thought a person in love ought to look. And I wanted to feel happy too, for her sake, but Davy was muttering beside me and everybody in back of us was saying sh-h-h, and we couldn't see, either, and altogether it put me into a complete feeze.

When we came out of the theater, the streets were full of people singing and blowing horns and not going anywhere, and there were searchlights slicing around in the sky and the buildings were full of lights and there were bells ringing in all the towers. It made you want to run and not care who you bumped into, even if it was some one you didn't know, only somehow it seemed as though

67

you knew everybody if you could only think of their name. I just stood there right in the middle of Broad Street, smiling at everybody, until Davy rudely pushed me on across ahead of a couple of cars that were swooping down on us.

"Look out, half-wit," he said; "do you want to go home with a leg under your arm?"

"See if I care," I said, skipping along. "It kind of crushes a girl to be out with a person that never thinks about anything but getting run over."

"Well, which do you want to be crushed by," Davy said, plowing up to the Ritz door, "me or some truck?" He guffawed loudly. "Why didn't you laugh, Maudie?"

"I was afraid if I started, I'd have hysterics," I said coldly, trying to get into the revolving door without getting chewed up.

"But that was good, darn it," Davy yelled. "That was funny."

"Was it?" I said with hauteur, only Davy gave the door a push and my section hit me in the back and I practically exploded into the lobby of the Ritz where everybody was. It was too embarrassing.

"Keep your shirt on, little girl," Hubie said, stopping me before I could stop him. "You got lots of time." Everybody simply howled with laughter, and in my soul I hated them all, except

68

Ting. It was pretty grim to think what her life was going to be like, if she really did ever marry this looloo, who besides everything else smelt like a can of Sterno. Honestly, he had a breath like a tiger.

Davy felt so awful when he saw what happened that I got feeling quite kindly toward him.

"Are you mad, Maudie?" he said as we went downstairs to the grille.

"No, I'm not mad," I said gently, "I just wish you'd behave, that's all."

The grille was crowded with people and tables and waiters — it looked as if we couldn't get in but we did. It was like getting on the subway at five o'clock, only worse, because food kept going in and out on trays and in case anything happened we were all underneath. When we finally got to our table, I felt like I'd been drawn through a keyhole. And when I turned around and saw Hubie sitting beside me, I about choked.

"Am I by you?" I said, not being able to believe my eyes.

"You are now," he said, smiling his famous smile, but I remained cold. "I wanted to see more of you."

"Did you move our cards?"

"Guilty, Your Honor," he said and laughed loudly.

"Gosh," I said. "Didn't Ting mind?"

"Ting has to humor me," he said, putting his arm around Ting. "As who doesn't?"

Everybody thought that was awfully funny, all but me and Davy. Even Ting laughed and laughed. Davy was right. She was in love, and I felt so sad, thinking how blind love makes a person. Here was Hubie acting so unattractive that how could anybody think he was much? I felt very mean, having those kind of thoughts when I was a friend of Ting's, because I suppose everybody wants other people to think the man they are in love with is wonderful, but it was pretty hard to see anything special in Hubie.

There were quite a few people on the party. Davy's and Ting's father and mother and some uncle and aunt named Mr. and Mrs. Jayne were at a little table, and at ours there was a man everybody called Chip and a man with a black mustache and Sylvia and Dora Ewing and us. Dora was looking hurt. I think she was next to Hubie before he changed the cards. Dora's the kind of a person who's almost a gloom, she's so introspective.

"How about robbing the cradle that-away, Hube?" said Chip, pointing his cigarette at me. "You ought to be ashamed, you with the bald head."

"Hubie isn't really bald," Ting said.

"Let it pass," Hubie said, blowing cigarette smoke all over everybody. "Grass don't grow on a busy street. Nor on a race track either," he added, looking around for applause.

Ting and Dora and Sylvia laughed eagerly and you could see they thought Hubie was too divine, and he sat there sort of preening his feathers. Honestly, it was perfectly sickening to see anybody that hated themself so.

"Did you hear that, Ting?" Dora said, still laughing. "I'll bet somebody's going to have their hands full making Hubie behave."

Ting just smiled in a pleased way and took a sip of water and rattled the ice in her glass. You could see she wasn't worrying. Love is so blind! The music started and out of the corner of my eye I saw Hubie turning toward me, after taking a big swallow out of a glass of ginger ale he'd been leaning under the table with.

"Yes, I'd adore to, Davy," I said, jabbing Davy with my elbow, thus jumping his grapefruit into his windpipe. "I'd adore to," I went on, kicking him in the ankle and stepping on his foot.

"Stop pushing me around," Davy complained, trying to pat himself on the back. "Where do you think you are — the Arena?"

"You're a big help, you are," I said scornfully, as we writhed through the struggling people on the

71

floor. "You're all talk. I despise people that are all talk."

"What do you mean, all talk?"

"Never mind," I said, "you wouldn't understand if I told you. That Hubie is all wet."

"That's what I been telling you," Davy said in wounded tones, and then a dreamy smile crept over his face. "Stale fellow, well wet. Did you get that, Maudie? Stale fellow, well wet."

Davy can really be as clever as anything when he tries.

"Here come the heavenly twins," Hubie sang out, as we came back to where our food was getting cold on our plates. "How long have you kept this hidden at home, Sylvia? Holding out on us, I call it."

"Oh, Maudie's only sixteen," Sylvia said languidly. "This is her big night. You know," she waved her fork with a piece of chicken on it, "peeping into life to see how wicked it all is."

I looked across at Sylvia and smiled my quiet smile.

"Really," I said with poise, buttering my roll. "I came out of curiosity. I heard there was going to be a man along who was in love with Ting. Nobody is actually good enough for her, but I was just curious to see somebody who thought they were."

72

"Oh, Lord," said Sylvia, "the crush again."

"Ouch!" said Hubie, and everybody laughed — except Ting, who looked at me reproachfully and patted Hubie's hand.

"Oh, awrrk," Davy gagged in my ear.

"There's one girl you can't make any time with, Hube," said the man with the black mustache. "I'd like to have that conversation framed."

Hubie leaned over and patted my roll, I having casually taken away my hand.

"Sister Maudie likes me," he said, taking an awful lot for granted. "She and I are going to be great friends. That's all girls are going to be to me from now on — just friends — with one exception," and he looked soulfully at Ting.

"At last, the one-woman man!" Chip said, and Dora laughed.

"Imagine Hubie going monogamous on us," she said.

"Well, a lot of husbands would sleep a lot easier if you once got hooked, Hube," Chip said.

"Hooked, heavens," Ting said, leaning forward earnestly. "That is a terribly cynical way to talk about love. I think love should be romantic, with both people not being able to live without each other and getting married because they want to."

"At-a-girl," Hubie said, putting his arm around

73

her, and then casually putting his other arm around me, only I threw it back in his face.

"Tut, tut," he said, "why so rough?"

"Nothing," I said, looking calmly at his arm around Ting, "only this is a one-way street."

"Well," he said, sort of moving his arm to see if it was all there, "you ought to put out your hand when you stop."

Well, everybody at the table simply howled. I just wished Sylvia could see how her chin ran down into her neck when she laughed. Everybody howled except Ting, that is. Her face got red and she started to say something, but just that minute the music started and everybody dashed out on the dance floor, seeming as though their chicken and peas had got them all pepped up.

"It's you and me this time, little one," Hubie said, sweeping me into his arms and up against his stomach, evidently expecting me to feel flattered. "Cutest little trick I ever hope to see," he said, holding me tighter. "And to think it's been buried in school — this immortal youth and beauty right here in my arms."

Well, I had no desire to be some stockbroker's Peter Pan, and I certainly didn't kind of like the whole thing anyhow.

"Do you know," I said casually, "I don't like you a bit."

"And can it scratch?" Hubie said, eyeing me coyly. "You don't know me, little girl. All I need is a little encouragement to show my best side."

"When I was little," I said, feeling myself getting curvature of the spine from leaning over backward away from his breath, which was strong enough by this time to turn handsprings on, "I was taught there wasn't such a thing as company manners, because if a person really had good manners they had them all the time. I think that's true of a person's best side."

"And can it philosophize?" Hubie said, bending over me. "Sixteen is a wonderful age. I wish I was sixteen."

"I wish you would lean on your own dinner," I said, "instead of mine."

He drew away.

"Maudie!" he said, "you disillusion me."

"Why should I care?" I said. "Do you know you're just so much dead wood to me, that I'd love to saw off and burn up."

The smile was gradually fading off of Hubie's face. Several people crashed into us and the orchestra blared in what was meant to be a challenge to the good old jungle blood, but it takes more than that music to make a monkey out of me.

"I guess you think you are experience coming into people's life. Well, I've had plenty of experi-

75

ence already — I just pretend to be naïve — and any time I want more, I know where I can get it — and you won't be it."

"Brother Davy will oblige, I suppose?" Hubie said, his eyes all narrowed down, but just then the music stopped and every one shouldered their way back to their tables, where several people were beginning to blow horns and wear paper hats.

"Maudie's a wild girl," Hubie said to our party. "Hey! hey! she likes to be."

"Don't be silly, Maud," Sylvia said. "Imagine Maud getting a chance to be wild."

Hubie leered at me. "You great big little stay-out-late," he said, patting my head, "I hope you get rained on sometime."

Well, from this point on the party was something to bury, as far as I was concerned. It got nearer and nearer to midnight and people got noisier and less like people until I just looked around and thought: Is this the human race? Mr. Jayne was wearing a yellow bonnet and blowing one of those things that uncurls into some one's ear and squeaks, and Mrs. Jayne was laughing and laughing so her chins rippled like little waves and there was confetti all over her bosom — she has one of those lullaby bosoms — and the ladies at the next table were putting nuts down one man's collar. I thought about Mother telling me how older people would

76

expect me to have good manners, and I wondered what was the big idea. We stopped throwing bread when I was fourteen.

It was ten minutes of twelve when all the lights went out except a red one that went round and round inside the bass drum. I was dancing with Chip when somebody's arm separated us and there was Hubie. His face was much redder than the last time I saw him; he really looked a little sprung.

"Nobody loves me any more," he roared into my ear, "not even you."

I didn't say anything. What was there to say?

"Come on, let's duck this party, kiddo," he said, "and sit out somewhere until the mob scene fades."

I started to throw hay on that idea, but somebody crashed into us and just about jarred my teeth loose, and somebody else ground their heel into my instep and tore my dress and I decided anything — even sitting out with Hubie — would be better than being torn limb from limb in the name of pleasure. If I had only realized that I was playing with fire — and that when you play with fire somebody else's fingers may get burnt. . . .

We went into the little hall and I sat down on the bottom step.

"Not there, cutie," Hubie said, "I like it cozy."

"I don't," I said, not moving.

77

Just then the orchestra played "Auld Lang Syne," and everybody screamed and cheered and the lights got green and then yellow and then blue and then all mixed up, and there was a big electric-light sign saying "Happy New Year" in the middle of the room. And before I could bite or kick, Hubie had wound his arms around me and was kissing me with his face, all hot and sticky, next to mine. Then the lights went up and there was Ting and the man with the black mustache standing in the door, looking at us.

"Just seeing the New Year in, Ting," Hubie said, with a nonchalant wave of the hand. "Gotta kissa girl to see the New Year in." His tongue sort of stumbled a little.

Ting gave him one freezing look. "So I see," she said and turned her back on us.

"Oh, forget it," he said, shrugging his shoulders. "Need a drink?"

"No," Ting said, "and neither do you, I should say." She turned to the man with the black mustache, who had been trying to make himself small in the background, and slipped her hand in his arm.

"Ting — " I said, but she didn't look back.

"Come on, let's dance, darling," she said to the man with the black mustache. "After all, this is — Happy New Year."

78

The way she said it, with a sort of a drawl, it sounded like "Sappy New Year", and that was about right, I thought, what with everybody acting so sappy at supper and Hubie being such a terrible sap. I was utterly disillusioned, and when I thought of how perfectly septic I must seem to Ting, my heart ached like a tooth. And as if that wasn't enough, Davy had been looking for me to see the New Year in with and when he discovered I'd been sitting out with Hubie, he acted very aloof for the rest of the evening and all the way home. I was too sunk to try to explain things to him, so I just lived on, feeling so low my tongue was practically dragging on the ground.

"Well," I said to myself, as I crawled into bed, "now you've buttered your bread, you can lie on it." I am naturally philosophical.

It seemed like the darkest hour actually was just before the dawn like you read about, though, because on New Year's morning, at what seemed like dawn, some one banged on my door just as I was trying not to wake up to the cold world of reality, and Sylvia stalked in, clutching her wrapper around her.

"Maud, Davy's here, for heaven's sake," she said, in a sleepy complaining voice, "honking his horn in the drive when it's only half-past eight. I could wring his neck."

79

I sat up. It was snowing and you could see your breath right in the room. Sylvia's nose was red.

"All right," I said, reaching around with my toe for my mules.

"Well, I wish you'd do something," Sylvia said crossly. Sylvia is not at her best before breakfast and she knows it and it affects her disposition. I am one of those rare people who look rather lovable, even after they've been asleep. So I just put on my evening cloak that was lying over the chair from last night over my pajamas and leaned out the window.

"Hello, big noise," I yelled over the honking of the horn. "Haven't you heard? This is to-morrow."

Davy stuck his head out the side of the car and looked up. "Hi, Maudie," he said, all smile, "Happy New Year."

"If that's what you got me out of bed at this ungodly hour for," I said, starting to close the window, "good-by, please."

"Hey, stupid, wait a minute!" Davy jumped out of the car and ran over under my window just like Romeo. "Say, wait a minute, can't you, Maudie? This is important."

"Well, what?" I said, pushing the window up again. Davy stood there a minute, looking up at me.

"Can't you come on down?" he said, scratching

his head and looking around. "It seems pretty intimate to go yelling all my private affairs up at a window."

"It would be much more intimate if I was down there in the snow in my night clothes," I said, idly brushing an icicle off on Davy.

"What's that fur thing you have on?" Davy said, peering at me.

"This?" I said airily. "Oh, this is just my fur pajamas. It's keeping body and soul together here for me in this open window."

"Gee, I'm sorry," Davy said, sucking the end of the icicle. "Gee, I'm an awful sap anyway, Maudie. I'll bet you think I'm the most terrible sap in the world, don't you, Maudie?" He looked very depressed.

"Why, Davy!" I said gently, but he went on.

"I didn't catch on a bit — I just thought well, I don't know what I thought, but I never thought you were framing Hubie like you did. Gee, Maudie, I think you're wonderful."

Well, my head was going round and round, trying to figure this out, and my eyes practically fell out on the snow, they were so amazed. Davy had been such a terrible scowl when he brought me home, and now look at him. I just thought to myself, anybody that can stay mad at me has got a pretty terrible disposition.

"I'm not so wonderful, Davy," I said modestly, knowing Davy would never believe me. "Anyhow, what's happened to Hubie?"

"Ting's aired him," Davy said, his voice breaking with joy. "Out on his ear. All because she saw him kissing you and realized what a two-timer he is. Gosh, Maudie, when I think of you sacrificing yourself to save my family — well, gosh!"

As I looked at Davy, I realized that I was his ideal. And I said to myself, what is the use of being a person's ideal if you can't let them have a few illusions about things?

"If you'll just wait until I put on my galoshes," I said, drawing my evening cloak around my pajamas, "I'll be down."

IV

LITTLE SISTER

IT WAS an awful slow party. Everybody was laughing around and saying cute things about being wallflowers, and the boys that were there were looking quite tired. I'm not exactly a bleak peony myself, but after fifteen minutes of Bill without a cut-in I was feeling rather fed up and had just suggested that we sit down before we fell down when somebody said, "Please may I break?" and I found myself surrounded by a perfect stranger. I knew he was a stranger because we don't say, "Please may I break?" in Philadelphia but "May I cut in?" or mostly nothing.

"Thanks horribly," I called after Bill. "Gosh, it was deevine." Hypocrite.

"Hello," said my savior.

"Hello," I said. "How did you get in?"

He looked quite surprised.

"Why," he said, "I was invited."

"No, you weren't," I said. "People your age have outgrown this class. It's Connie Duveyn's coming-out party that you belong at; that's upstairs in the Rose Garden."

"Say," he said, "you have a knack for making people feel at home. Am I as bad as all that?"

He had long thin eyes and hair growing quite far back on his head. He was tall, too, and thick in an inspiring way.

"I didn't mean to offend you," I said, with a rather attractive worried look. "But debutantes' friends are apt to be bored with dancing-class children, and I was wondering if maybe you hadn't come quite a distance for Connie's party."

He smiled down at me and wrapped his arm around me in a more or less affectionate way. Sylvia has mentioned that particular method of dancing. I didn't know exactly what to do. I didn't want to do anything much.

"Connie has more men than she can possibly use," he said, "and she isn't apt to miss me. Frankly, I was on my way home and I decided to look in.

84

I didn't know exactly what to do.

Then I saw you and couldn't help breaking in. Do you think I was fresh?" He looked awful fresh and perfectly ideal. I bet he was fresh.

"Did you feel fresh?" I asked naïvely.

He thought that was rather good. "You don't think I ought to go?"

"Don't go!" I said earnestly. "I was just praying for you to happen."

He seemed to like that. I must have looked rather sweet when I said it.

"Come in and talk to me," he said, eying the empty supper room. "This party is just about to lie down and die, anyhow." I looked timid. Bill passed me steering Julie Purviance in scallops around the edges of parents and gold chairs. There was something eternal in the way Julie fell over his toe every time they turned. And just then it occurred to me that I had been too good ever since I was born.

"You don't know my name, you know," I reminded him, as he turned our chairs with the backs to the door.

"Oh, don't I? What will you give me if I do?"

"How'd you find out?"

"There's lots of things I know — never mind how. Didn't you know you were famous? As a matter of fact, I came down to the Duveyn brawl

87

specially to see Sylvia, and then found out that she was in Europe. Perhaps you've heard her speak of me?" he asked hopefully. "I'm Wellington Coxe."

I should think I had. Sylvia hadn't talked about any one else since the prom where she'd met him. He was a Junior at Princeton, Number 6 on the crew, Ivy Club, and sang one of his own songs in the Triangle. Just a girl's dream come to life. And more than that, he was the answer to a parent's prayer. Most of his ancestors seemed to have fought in the Revolution and his father was president of a rather important bank somewhere. He was the one friend of Sylvia's that the family had ever called suitable, and you can see how hard she'd fallen for him when I tell you that even this hadn't stopped her ravings.

I realized that God had given my better nature a chance to do a good deed, even if I had been asked to resign from the Girl Scouts, but just in time I remembered our class motto: "Every Girl for Herself." I could tell this too perfectly superb man that Sylvia was pash about him and he'd probably remain faithful to her until she got home, but why should I? After all, I was stuck in school while she was having herself a time in Europe, and she hadn't even raised a finger to get the family to take me along.

88

I gave Wellington a blank look. "I'm sorry," I said sweetly, "I don't believe I have."

"That's a woman for you," he said bitterly. "Stringing me along to think I was a big moment in her life and it was all a line. If she'd cared at all, she'd at least have let me know she was going to be away for a couple of months."

I knew Sylvia had wanted to let him know terribly but was afraid he'd think she was rushing him. She'd only just met him, and he'd said he was coming to see her but hadn't yet.

"There are so many men in Sylvia's life," I said casually. Then I changed the subject with my most adorable smile. "But there aren't very many in mine," I said. "There hasn't been time."

I could see that he thought I was terribly cute. His arm slid over the back of my chair. "They told me upstairs that you could ease my pain," he said, "and I think maybe they were right."

Then they played "Good Night, Ladies," everybody feeling rather old and tired, and I vanished artfully into the crowd. I have a habit of not boring people. Sylvia says it is my greatest asset.

Sylvia says that her idea of hell is one long Sunday afternoon listening to bores. She was telling me about it one night, after she and Arthur Dear had been talking for one or two hours about how they make felt hats in Arthur Dear's father's fac·

tory. Sylvia has lots of men friends, but they do talk to her about felt hats. That's one thing about boys in school. They can't tell you all about soap and how it's made or something. But Sylvia's men propose, too; in fact, I am almost sure that is why Mother and Father took her to Europe. Well, I bet she marries a Frog. Wellington calls them Frogs.

I wonder why they are called Frogs. I asked Welly but he didn't seem to know.

"Why are your New Haven friends called Bulldogs?" he said attractively. "They aren't, you know."

Aunt Benevolence was rather inhospitable when he first arrived. After all, it was early. About nine o'clock the next morning the doorbell rang and to my intense astonishment it was him.

"Hello," he said. "Nice girl — try to run away from a fellow. I hope you had bad dreams."

I sat down on the umbrella stand. Aunt Benevolence had stopped munching her health wheat and was flattened out against the back of her chair so that she could give us a cold eye out the dining-room door.

"I didn't seem to do a very good job of it," I said. My smile felt stiff. I wished I had remembered to put cold cream on it the night before.

"You did very well," he said. "But now you

and I are going for a ride, if she of the fishy eye —
how about making her used to me?"

"No," I said. I wasn't taking any chances with
Aunt Benevolence. She has no reserves. She'll talk
about her liver or her intestinal flora or gas even,
with almost perfect strangers. "I'm late now. We're
only going to ride two blocks to where — where I
go to school."

"School? Oh, good Lord! Do you have to go to
school?"

"Yes," I said unpleasantly, "don't you?"

"Not to-day. I'm cutting my math." Then he
tucked me gently into his roadster and asked me
would I have lunch with him.

It wasn't until the ice cream — in tall silver
things with ice, like they had at Sylvia's coming-
out party — that I remembered that Welly — I'd
got to calling him Welly by then — was really
Sylvia's man.

"Too bad I'm not Sylvia," I said languidly.
"How bored you must be."

"Do you really think so?" His hand sort of accidentally dropped over mine. I looked bashful. I
look rather lovable that way. He leaned forward
and gave me an intense burning look. "Now I have
a feeling," he said, "that I'm going to like you best
— of all my girls, I mean. After all, there has to
be a best, doesn't there?"

"I may be best for you," I looked down demurely, "but do you think you'll be good for me?" I was really too good to be true.

"I'll certainly try," he said. "Here's 'Love is Fun.' Shall we dance?"

Well, dancing with Welly was like going to a few rather important football games with anybody else, and I wished Sylvia could have seen me. It made me laugh just to think of Arthur Dear, for instance. If I could have known that the bitter day was coming when I should cry at the mere thought of Welly — and not be able to think of anything else. . . .

"Funny thing," he said, when the music stopped for a while, "I didn't used to get any kick out of dancing. I remember once I wore cleats to dancing class so the girls would be afraid of my feet."

"How simply screaming," I said, airily waving my coffee cup. "If that's the way you feel, you better run along back to Princeton and study your algebra — I mean trigonometry."

Welly leaned front on his elbows and pulled the corner of my silk neckerchief.

"Listen, Maudie" — it was the first time he'd called me Maudie — he said, looking positively enchanting, "how about letting my college career take care of itself, and you and I — "

"You're leaning on your cake," I said, "and it's goo-ing."

Aunt Benevolence once told me that love was the seed of beauty, which may or may not be true, because Welly is quite lovely looking in a satisfying way. I thought about him the next day in church. Davy smiled at me after every hymn. To think there was a time when I thought he was quite exciting!

We got a cable from Father saying, "Love all well", or something like that, and Aunt Benevolence put twenty-five cents extra in the collection for preservation on the great deep. I didn't put in anything but said a prayer for the poor instead, as I had already spent the ten dollars Father gave me at parting. I was glad Aunt Benevolence didn't notice because she is always saying, "Extra works, extra grace." But I'll bet you can't buy off the Lord like that, anyway.

I thought about religion quite frequently that week. After all, I daresay it depends on what sin you commit as to exactly how wicked you are, and honestly I didn't feel wicked about wolfing Sylvia's man. Perhaps if I could have looked into the future and seen myself sitting in the cold gray dusk, chewing the end of my hair with an aching heart, I might have felt different.

Welly telephoned long-distance from Princeton

93

one night. "Say," came faintly over the wire, "say, is that you? Can you hear me, Maud? Helluva connection! How about to-morrow afternoon? I'll be down on the two-fifty-eight — hope you haven't got a date. You have? Bet you're stuffing me. All right, eight o'clock, then? What?"

I always hang up a little unexpectedly.

Welly was one of those people who left you wondering what would have happened if he had stayed longer, and made you wish you had the courage to find out. It's perfectly natural, I suppose, for women to be drawn to men — even Aunt Benevolence has her favorite postman. And though Julie Purviance always says she has no spiritual contact point with men, I suspect it's because she steps on their feet. Men have to draw the line somewhere. But Welly never seemed to notice how far he was leading you, which made me realize with a certain tolerance that whatever he did he did innocently.

"The aunt out to-night?" he said, laying his hat on the card tray.

"No," I said, "she's in bed. I'm sorry."

"I'm not," Welly was nothing if not frank; "she chills me."

"Try to be polite," I reproved him.

"I can't help being perfectly frank," he said. "It makes me a great many enemies, but some real

94

friends too." Was he funning me? I wondered. I seemed to remember saying something like that to him once. Then he changed the subject. "Ever been out on the Boulevard at night?"

"No," I said; "is it different out there?"

"You wonderful kid," he said. "I wonder how much you know."

I thought of me helping myself into Davy's fliver, especially the time it had snowed all over the seat. After all, they might have taken me to Europe.

It was quite late when we got home.

I had Aunt Benevolence right under my thumb and Welly was eating out of my hand by this time, inviting me to proms and things, and life was getting as smooth as a chocolate frap. It's a funny thing about life. Whenever things get going too good, you can just know that Fate is going to come along and sock you in the eye.

Mary Brandt had an Easter house party in the Poconos about six weeks after I met Wellington. I felt rather sunk when I left, because it meant that I couldn't see Welly that weekend, and then I couldn't find my powder and I didn't have time to buy any, and I don't like to use tooth powder too often because it hurts my nose. It shows too. Aunt Benevolence was feeling neglected about being left alone — particularly as she was having one of her attacks — and hoped I'd have what pleasure I could, which made me feel a little aloof. And when we got to Pocono it was raining.

It occurred to me, as we were playing "Up Jenkins", that I had rather outgrown Mary. It seemed awful immature to hear the boys talking about college-board exams and how Chestnut Hill Academy might beat Penn Charter. I dropped the quarter twice and Davy said cleverly, thinking I was still crazy about him, "How about holding it next time, Maud?"

"How about holding it yourself, Davy?" I said. "It seems to mean so much more to you."

Every one looked slightly shocked, but Davy just smiled his smile and said, "Ha! Ha!" in what he thought was gruelling irony.

Everybody laughed cautiously and I said with a graceful yawn, "Oh, grow up, Davy." It just wilted Davy.

I felt rather good until Mary said in that sweet way girls have when they're pumping each other. "How was Princeton, Maud?"

Now I hadn't told any one about Welly because I didn't want any competition. I personally don't think any of them have quite my charm, but I felt that here was one place where I could treat myself to a little safety, and I thought nobody knew I was at the prom. For a minute I couldn't think of any way of crumbling Mary until a casual saying of Sylvia's happened into my head.

"Very nice," I said in Sylvia's tone, "as proms go."

Just about then the telephone ran long-distance and it was for me. I felt rather weak. It looked like it usually does in my life — as though everything was going to happen at once, which it promptly did.

"Maud? Hello, kid, this is Welly. Listen, how do you get to Pocono from the Bethlehem Pike?"

I didn't know, but when he arrived, he spent quite a few minutes outlining the various kinds of dumbness that had paved the way.

"Nobody in this damn State," he said, stuffing his cap into the pocket of the car, knows the Delaware from the Susquehanna. One fellow communed with me for ten minutes with the sun in his eyes and thought he was facing north. And cold! My Lord!"

I felt rather annoyed in a pleasant way.

"It's funny," I said, "but I don't seem to get the same thrill out of seeing you that I usually get."

He stopped and looked down at me divinely.

"How do you mean?" he said.

"Well," I said, "in the first place you're boring me." I eyed him with an expression of ennui.

He felt awful about it, the way I meant him

97

to, and we strolled into the empty living room where there were a lot of rabbits and eggs and things. Really it had been an awful tame party. Welly sat down and began to peel the ear off of Mary's rabbit.

"I just had to see you," he said.

"So I supposed," I said, in a discouraging way. "You certainly seemed awfully glad to see me." A man takes a girl at her own valuation and I wasn't going to let Welly think he could take his peeve out on me. It wasn't my fault that the place was inaccessible to get to.

He looked unhappy. "I know," he said, "sorry." He stamped on the rabbit and tore his hair.

"Say, Welly," I said. "What's the matter with you, anyway?"

It was getting kind of silly — me watching him be harassed.

"Are you alone?" he asked, without much sense.

"I look it, don't I?"

"This house feels full of people to me. Come on out in the car — how about it? I've got to talk to you."

My spine quivered gently. I felt like a person that is living on a firecracker.

"Can you say it by five o'clock? They'll be back from Big Bear by then."

In looking back, I remember that my coat wasn't

98

warm enough and I had gotten a letter from Sylvia saying she had just lost eleven dollars at Monte Carlo. I couldn't remember when I had felt so depressed.

"Maud," said Welly, "are you warm enough?"

"No," I said unhappily.

There was a little silence during which Welly ran over a chicken. We turned up a place where there used to be a road and stopped.

"Maudie," said Welly, his eyes kind of beating the air, "will you — won't you — give me a kiss?"

I thought a moment.

"Would I be warmer then?" I said.

It's funny, but that seemed to be too much for Welly. I hadn't realized how irresistible I could be, even in a sweet, unprovocative dress.

"You're so adorable," he murmured passionately, when he finally came up for air.

Before I could say anything he again closed over my head, kissing me rather violently.

After a while he asked me to wear his Ivy pin. The night before I was playing "Up Jenkins" and listening to little bright sayings about the Lawrenceville game and how the Sixth Form didn't take Virgil, and here I was having a varsity crew man kissing me in the Poconos and talking about me wearing his Ivy pin. I bet that's what they call life.

"To-morrow," Welly whispered, as we turned in the drive, "you'll drive home with me, honey?" It was seven o'clock and Mary came peering out on the porch.

"Don't you see I can't, darling?" I said. "But I'll call you up the minute I get home," I promised.

Mary was quite irritated. I'd told her I was feeling a little tired.

"Well, Maud," she said in a hurt way, "I'm glad you had a nice time."

"Yes," I said, "unexpected things can be nice sometimes." It didn't do any good, though. Girls are funny the way they enjoy having their feelings hurt.

"Was it the Princeton swain?" Davy asked with a smooth smile. I raised my eyes to his with a look full of sweetness.

"Yes," I said, "it was."

All the way home on Monday I thought about Welly in a romantic way — how he smiles over his nose and says, "Listen, kid," and doesn't part his hair. I liked to think about him kissing me. It was quite interesting thinking about love in an experienced way.

Life revolved in a lovely sort of a pink-and-gold haze for a couple of weeks and then we got a radiogram from Father saying, "Home Thursday love", or something like that. I didn't feel nearly so sure of Father's love as I once had.

I knew I was still a little child to Father even if I was sixteen. He hadn't even let me dance at Sylvia's ball — "Not yet awhile, little sister," he'd said; "plenty of time for balls when you're older." Will I ever forget the bitterness to me of those words? So what would he think of my having an affair with Welly, though how could I have helped it, with him pursuing me to the Poconos and everything? But it was sort of depressing to think that when Sylvia had affairs they took her to Europe, whereas, my being the youngest and quite small, discipline was apt to be quite humiliating to me when Father found out. Parents usually have one unloved child.

Then the family were home: Mother a nervous wreck from smuggling things through the customs and Father saying, "Well, well, it's a good thing to go away once in a while — makes you so glad to get home", and Sylvia sporting the latest shriek in French haircuts that she boasted the customs man had said she ought to pay duty on.

"Well, little sister, you've been good, I hope," Father asked and beamed when Aunt Benevolence said that I really was a sweet child. Sweet child! I looked down demurely. If they only knew. Welly was coming to take me to a hockey match the next afternoon and I had a premonition — well, there was nothing to do at this point but wait and let things blend.

As soon as she could get me off alone, Sylvia started handing me a lot of gore about a cute Frenchman with a mustache she'd met in Paris and the affair she'd had with him and all the affairs she'd had on the boat. I was really so bored I could hardly be civil. Somehow Sylvia's affairs didn't thrill me the way they used to before I knew about life from actual experience. I began thinking about Welly again. I hadn't really thought about him in a couple of hours, in all the excitement of the family getting home, and I felt kind of unfaithful to him.

The next afternoon when he came I could feel my face light up — I'll bet that's what a love light is. And then there was Sylvia before I had a chance to say anything to him.

"Hello, stranger," he said to her, at the same time giving my hand an intimate little squeeze.

"Well, if it isn't Wellington Coxe! You make coming home worth while," Sylvia gushed. "How did you know I was back?" She thought he had come to see her!

"I have a way of finding those things out — never mind how. Didn't you know you were famous?" Welly played right up to her.

This sort of airy banter went on for awhile without my saying much and then Sylvia asked what it was like out. I saw through her little ruse. She wanted to get rid of me by having Welly take her out for a ride.

"Bit of a drizzle," Wells said, not catching on.

"Bad for waved hair," I said, looking meaningly at Sylvia's French bob. My hair is naturally curly. "And that reminds me, Welly," I went on casually, "if we're going to get to that game on time, we'd better start."

"Right you are," Welly said, jumping up. "Be seeing you soon, Sylvia." And we started off.

I smiled over my shoulder and saw Sylvia throwing an epileptic. In that moment she hated me, I know. I'll bet she was hoping my step-ins would fall off or something.

The hockey was quite exciting. There were two or three players hurt and Welly and I had a perfectly marvy time. We parked for a while afterward, so it was quite late when we got home and I had to say good-by to Welly at the door without asking him in. I hated to let him go — I always did, of course, but particularly this time. My insides had a deserted feeling when I thought of the dirt Sylvia had probably been dishing the family about me.

There they all were in the library — Mother

and Father and Sylvia — and not a kind word or a smile from any of them as I came in. A cold chill curled my spinal cord and my voice had a sort of gulp in it as I said nonchalantly, "Where's the body?" It's so hard to be nonchalant when you're not allowed to smoke.

Not a rise from anybody. I could see I was in for a grim experience.

"Maud," Mother said, clearing her throat in that little way she has that sounds like some one sharpening a knife, "Sylvia tells me that Wellington Coxe was here this afternoon."

"Yes," I said.

"I'm sorry you didn't call me."

"Welly will be crushed," I said, "but we had to get to the game."

"I don't like your way of speaking to your Mother, Maud," Father said, "and from what I have managed to find out from Benevolence, you have been taking advantage of our absence to behave in a way that I don't approve of in the least. We may as well be frank."

"Let's," I said, looking at Sylvia, who was gazing out the window at some dead grass which the beetles ate.

"I understand from your aunt that you went to a dance at Princeton, knowing, as you did, my feelings on the subject of fifteen-year-old girls — "

I took off my beret with dignity and laid it on the table.

"I am sixteen, Father," I said, "and, Mother, it seems to me that when I show the good judgment to fall for the one man you've ever called suitable, you and Father might give me a little credit instead of kicking me around like a — like a football."

"Suitable for Sylvia," Mother said firmly. There's no getting the better of Mother in an argument and I knew it, but I couldn't help going on trying. After all, my whole future happiness was at stake.

"It's not my fault if Welly prefers me, is it?" I looked at the tears rolling unattractively around Sylvia's nose. "And I don't blame him." Then I felt the tears rolling unattractively around my own nose. It was all so intense and tragic.

Mother's heart was as cold as dry ice. "You're entirely too young to be carrying on with Wellington Coxe," she said. "That's final."

Suddenly it was all clear to me. Even if Welly was still in college, Mother was building for the future. She wanted to marry Sylvia off to him while I went right on going to school.

"All right," I said, "arrange your marriage of convenience. But let me give you fair warning. Welly's devoted to me and I to him, and if I'm sep-

arated from the man I love — I'll elope with him."
I left the room dramatically.

I got to my room somehow and then collapsed
on the bed and cried and cried. My emotions felt
as though they had been run through a meat
grinder. Pretty soon I heard Father call, "Dinner's
ready, Maudie." I didn't answer.

A little bit later he called again, "There's fried
bananas, Maudie." I am passionately fond of fried
bananas.

"Don't want any," I called back. I went on crying and for a long time there was silence. I guess
they were all busy eating the fried bananas.

I just lay there, feeling simply sunk. Things
couldn't of been worse. There I was with my heart
in bits, ignored and forgotten by the family and
literally starved. That was mean of Father to tell
me about the fried bananas. Even the thought of
all those idyllic days with Welly didn't help any.
They seemed to have been years and years ago.
And thinking of Welly made me think of how I'd
threatened to elope with him. And I'd do it, too,
if the family tried to stop me from seeing him.
And then I'd be married and couldn't have a coming-out ball like Sylvia's. I started to cry again.

Then there was a knock on the door. I didn't
answer, just sobbed a little louder. "I had a hot
plate saved for you, Maudie. Don't you think you

could eat something if I had it sent up?" It was Father, sounding very worried.

I thought a minute. "No," I said and went on sobbing.

"May I come in then?" Father asked timidly.

"I don't care," I said into the pillow. Nothing mattered to me any more.

Father came in and sat on the edge of my bed and tried to pat me soothingly on the shoulder, but I didn't feel like being soothed. I shook his hand off. "Do you really feel so bad about it?" he asked.

"I w-wish I was d-dead," I choked out between sobs. "I'll never love anybody like Welly."

Father didn't say anything for a long time. I peeked at him and he looked quite distraught. I sobbed a little harder. That was too much for Father. "Don't cry like that, Maudie," he begged. "Please don't." I let him pat my shoulder but I didn't entirely stop crying.

"I have an idea," Father said.

I stopped crying but didn't speak.

"I've been thinking," Father went on, "how nice Florida is at this time of year. My business doesn't really need me right now. Suppose you and I go down there for a month on a little junket of our own — just we two. How about it, Maudie?"

I sat up, weak but smiling.

V

A HUSBAND FOR SYLVIA

MOTHER's schemes didn't work out though, because, when I got back from Palm Beach with the most marvelous winter tan you've ever seen and very sophisticated, Welly was nowhere in sight. Sylvia had let him get away. Honestly that girl gives me an ache sometimes, the way she gets all the breaks and still it don't get her anywhere. And as though it wasn't enough for Mother to make me give up Welly just because she wanted him for a husband for Sylvia, and then have Sylvia lose him out of the family entirely, what should I hear but Sylvia and Mother putting my friends on the pan.

"The worst thing about Davy is his ears," Sylvia

was saying complainingly. "They look like fungus."

"Now, Sylvia," Mother said. "This list will be impossible to fill in, if you're going to be absurd. I suggested Chi Carter — "

"He reminds me of a wet dog," Sylvia said unpleasantly. "The way he drips all over his collar in church. Honestly, Mother, I can't have some uncouth juvenile there with all these attractive people."

"Hush," Mother said in a muffled voice. "Here's Maudie."

I stood in the doorway, where I had practically jelled from shock, though usually I pride myself on my poise. Sylvia was spread out on Father's couch in her wrapper, while Mother wrote things down and crossed them out at the desk.

"What are you hashing over my intimate friends for?" I said with dignity.

"We're not, dumb-bell," Sylvia said brazenly. "We're trying to make a list for my table at the Junior League Dinner Dance."

"With my friends?" I asked.

"No, dear," Mother said in soothing tones. "Father and I agreed to take a table for Sylvia, only instead of getting her guests invited at once, she has let it go until a great many of her own friends are going to other tables."

109

"Mother, it's a wonder I have any time left for anything!" Sylvia interrupted, "with the whole Program Committee dumped on me just because Ting went to Europe and Janice is having a baby — "

"Sh! — " Mother said, looking at me.

"That's all right," I said gently. "I was a baby myself once."

"Dear, it's purely a question of filling places," Mother said in a squelching voice — I don't think Mother approves of the facts of life. "Sylvia needs two more men to fill the table, and she's simply considering the younger boys."

"Well, perhaps it's a good idea," I said, bouncing my squash ball back of Sylvia's head. "A little youth might pep the party up. I'll certainly like it better."

Sylvia sat up so suddenly that the heels of her mules banged on the floor.

"It doesn't matter what you think, idiot," she said, "you aren't going to be there."

"I was just wondering," Mother said, as I stared dumbly at Sylvia, not being able to believe my ears, "if we could use Mrs. Felton's nephew. She mentioned to me this afternoon that he would be with her this week, as he has business in Philadelphia."

"Probably some one else has got him," Sylvia said.

"I don't think so. I didn't see Mrs. Felton until five o'clock and she had just had the wire. Why don't you try, and then just use one of Maudie's friends for the other place?"

"What's his name?" Sylvia said from the telephone, "I ought to seem bright when I talk to Mrs. Felton."

"You could try," I said bitterly, "but I bet it won't be very convincing." And so I wouldn't spoil a super-crack like that by bursting into tears, which I was afraid I was going to, I turned haughtily on my heel and left. I felt my way blindly down the stairs, appalled as I realized that no matter how faithful a boy may be in his soul, he is sure to feel awfully flattered if some older girl makes a pass at him.

I sat down on the bottom step and thought what I could do to get Sylvia out of my life. The logical thing for a person who is not talented so they could go on the stage, or bright enough for business like being a typewriter, and who has a naturally rather brutal nature so they would not be too hot giving their lives to charity, is to get married. Sylvia and Mother had both been working on it, I had to admit, but it occurred to me that maybe I might be able to have a good idea. I went into the library where there is a comfortable sofa that I like to think on, but just as I was about to sink limply into it, I discovered Jerry there, reading Father's *Saturday Evening Post*.

I can't remember when Jerry hasn't been around our family. His family live over in Turkey or one of those places where there are so many natives and so few civilized people, and his father is the head of a hospital there. Jerry came over here when he was about twelve to go to school and college and everything, and now, even when he is in business, he still is around our house a lot. He used to spend his vacations with us and times like when he broke his leg, and week-ends, on account of our family and his family being so fond of each other, and naturally we are all very used to him.

"You don't look so happy," he said, dropping his legs on the floor to make room for me. "What's the matter?"

"I was just thinking," I said, "about love and marriage and motherhood, and what is Sylvia getting out of life, after all?"

A mental picture of Sylvia scooping up my intimate friends still swam before my unseeing eyes. I suddenly decided I needed Jerry for an ally, even if I couldn't explain to him the real reason why.

"Jerry," I went on, "Sylvia ought to be getting married. She isn't getting any younger, after all. She was nineteen last November."

Jerry suddenly started to put another log on

the fire, irregardless of the fact that there were four already and the fire was out.

"I was just thinking over the drips she goes with —"

"Like me," said Jerry.

"Oh, I don't mean you," I said with a kind smile, "you're different. I mean Hubie and Otis Boyer and Chip Dillworth — and you know. Just drips."

"Ye gods," Jerry said. "Don't be so forceful. They seem like pretty good scouts to me — no intellectual Hercules or anything but nice enough guys."

"When I get married," I said, "I marry a Leo man, and I bet I don't waste time over any Otis Boyer either."

"Otis'd be a nice fellow," Jerry said, "if you dried him off."

"You'd have to wring him out," I said firmly.

"Well, how about Hubie, then?" Jerry asked.

"He's been dead for years," I said. "They just haven't been able to get him to lie down." Jerry chortled in an appreciative way that is always very gratifying, even though what you've said isn't original. "What's the matter with you marrying Sylvia, Jerry? It would be so much easier. I mean, I'd just tell you and you could do it."

Jerry shook his head.

"Just as easy as that," he said. "No, I'm waiting

113

for you. I've been eating out my heart for ten years while you grew up."

That was the trouble with Jerry. Sylvia had to cross him off her list years ago because you can't get him to be serious.

"You're no help," I complained, kicking his foot, "and I'll bet just on the way things happen to Sylvia that she's up there now hooking another oogle."

"In her bedroom?" Jerry said, looking startled. I soothed him with a languid hand.

"On the 'phone. She's gunning for this Felton person who's coming — "

"Well, he's no drip," Jerry said emphatically. "I went to college with him. Ted's a darn good egg. He stroked our crew. And what he doesn't know about women — "

Dreamily I got up and turned on the phonograph with my favorite record. I think better when there is soft music playing.

"Would he do," I asked Jerry, while thoughtfully clogging, "for a husband for Sylvia?"

"Ideal," Jerry said. "Just the type."

Well, those were the most cheering words I had heard in several weeks, and I was even more cheered when Sylvia came down just as I was changing the needle, and said he could come. She didn't pay much attention to Jerry and he was reading, any-

114

way, so I found out a few important facts without interruption, which usually is practically impossible in this house.

"He's twenty-four," Sylvia said, turning off my favorite record and getting out some old graybeard like 'High and Low', "and he comes from Boston and he can't get there till nine o'clock. Goodness knows what he'll be like. Maudie, what makes that ghastly howl right in the best part of the record?"

"It's called a howler," I said. "Some new kind of a needle. Davy put it on last night and it sure did put zip into all the soft records. It's the only one Davy could get."

"That reminds me," Sylvia said, taking off the howler and throwing it in the fire. "I decided on Davy. He is the tallest and looks less like a frog than most of the juveniles. When do you think he'll be home, so I can call him?"

"Around six," I said placidly, knowing Davy always got home at five, so he could tune in on the hockey scores. Then I slid artfully into the hall, got my beret and my wind-breaker and went out the back door.

Davy only lives about a block from our house and I saw his model-T leaning up against the curb when I got there, so I went around on the lawn and banged on the window of the study where I could hear some smug radio voice talking. Nothing happened, so I banged again until I heard a little splitting sound which sounded as if the glass was probably broken.

"Hey, shut up!" Davy suddenly opened the window and shouted. "Shut up! Shut up! Quit busting — Oh, hello, Maudie. Do you want something?"

I climbed in the window and turned off the radio.

"Don't get up," I said coldly, eying Davy, who was sitting in the only comfortable chair, "you might have a heart attack. I love chivalry in a man."

"Well, how did I know you were going to ease through that window just as they were making a goal?" he complained, heaving himself out of the chair. "The whole point of listening to a game is to see who won."

"Listen," I said, sinking down on the arm, "and stop beefing. This is an emergency and I've got to have some co-operation. Sylvia is asking you to her dinner dance and I want you to tell her you won't come unless I'm there."

An evil gleam lit up Davy's face. It's sad the way men are usually bad at heart.

"Oh, I don't know," he said, "you aren't the only woman in my life."

I gave him a calm smile.

"Be subtle," I said, "you're just a means to an

end, a sort of a tool. And you aren't the only man in Sylvia's life either. She was considering Chi. All I have to do is throw a little weight — "

"Now don't go throwing your weight around," Davy said, laughing loudly, "all I want to know is, what is this all about? I don't want to go around compromising myself — I gotta look out for my interests."

"All right," I said, rising and brushing off the arm, "it's both of us or neither. If you don't insist on my being there, I'll tell Sylvia you have pink-eye." And I haughtily put my foot out the window.

"Check," Davy said, "check. I was only kidding, blond girl. What do I want to go around with a lot of hags for, I want to know, if you aren't there?"

"Davy," I said, pulling my other foot gently over the window sill, "it's men like you that make this world what it is." And I vanished into the dusk, leaving Davy's tender smile gradually fading into a look of uncertainty.

I was positively never so excited in my life as I was when we actually got to the dinner dance on Friday night. Everywhere you looked there were balloons — big red and yellow clusters swaying to and fro over people's heads; and here and there a stray one would go drifting by through the cig-arette smoke and the changing lights until you would hear a pop and there it would be, all shrivelled and stepped on, under people's feet. Our table was right on the edge of the dance floor, and when I looked up, the ceiling was so far away it made everybody look little and flat and pointless, with so much space over them.

"You're over there, Maud," Sylvia said, pointing to the chair which every tray of soup bumped as it went by, "and you're next, Davy. There ought to be eleven chairs — are there? Somebody count."

I was the eleventh and naturally it crowded the table. Even Davy was feeling a little unfriendly to me, in spite of my practically getting him invited, in a way. But just as everybody pulled in and sat down, upsetting everybody else's water, a tall figure came weaving through the other tables, and Jerry, who was sitting next to me on the other side, turned and sort of pointed with his eyes, the way you can and still be perfectly polite.

"There he is," he said. "The old hatchet-faced sorrel-top. Look him over."

From the way people at other tables were waving at him and shouting, I could see that he was something pretty special. He did have a thinnish face and hair a little the color of a flower-pot, but he was the sort of a person that all his features which might have been bad news for any ordinary person, just looked like lucky breaks on him. Sylvia's rather suspicious expression had melted into a pleased smile that ran all over her face, and she was enthusiastically pulling out the chair beside her and reaching out her arm in his direction. I noticed what I have so often noticed when girls wave gaily at attractive men in front of other girls, — their arm is very pretty but their hand looks like a claw, just unconsciously.

"It's so divine you got here," Sylvia greeted him passionately as he sat down, while flinging herself on one elbow on the table, with her shoulder blade just grazing Otis's ear, who was sitting on her other side. "I've been absolutely dying to meet you — I've heard so much about you!"

Just then the music started very loud and challenging and whether Sylvia ever really introduced anybody or not in all the din I couldn't tell, but the next thing I knew she and Ted were dancing off across the room, and Dora Ewing and Jane Carter and Nancy Harrison were looking rather sourly at Otis and Chip and Hubie, who were springing gaily to their feet and making snapping sounds with their fingers and wiggling their knees as though dancing with them was going to be one long thrill. I saw Sylvia's face getting a sickening expression of adoring wonder on it as she looked up at Ted that would be enough to drive him into the arms of another woman, and I realized that I would have to act quickly to keep Sylvia from getting off to a bum start, on account of a man's first impressions of you are so terribly important. Luckily some one bumped into them just then and mashed her sugary smile into his shirt.

"Jerry," I muttered, grabbing Jerry's sleeve, "go cut in on Sylvia, will you?"

"My gosh," Jerry said, brushing ashes off of himself, "look what you made me do. Get me a vacuum cleaner."

"Don't be funny," I said, shaking the back of his chair. "This is a crisis. Sylvia is out there ruining her life."

"What's the big idea, being so high hat?" Davy suddenly asked, appearing around the side of my impassioned back. "I asked you three times how about ankling out."

"Absolutely right," Jerry said. "Quit monopolizing me, Maudie, and ankle along. As a special favor to you, and because I was about to do it anyway, I'll go give Sylvia a thrill."

Well, I would have thrown Davy to the wolves then, if I could have, but I had to be content with knowing that Sylvia at least was being called in. I saw Ted walk back to our table and look around for a match. Then the music stopped just as Davy and I got across the floor and we saw Dora and Jane and Nancy appearing at the table out of everywhere, with Hubie and Otis and Chip trying to follow them and being bumped and jolted and looking very annoyed. Jerry and Sylvia slid in from somewhere back of the tables and sat down, and a waiter went weaving over with some chicken croquettes.

Davy grabbed me by the wrist.

"Step on it, blond girl," he yelled, much to my embarrassment, "we're missing the boat."

"Didn't you have any dinner?" I asked coldly, walking very dignified across the room among the last; "you should have brought that rubber hot dog of yours." Davy has a hot dog made out of rubber that he is always slipping into people's sandwiches when they're not looking.

When we got to our table, Jane and Dora and Nancy and Sylvia were all laughing and saying clever witticisms in that excited way that sometimes makes me wonder is any man worth it? I stood and looked at them all a minute before sitting down. It's very funny the way I don't get the jitters like most girls if I am standing up and everybody else is sitting down and looking at me. It really rests me, in a way. I suppose that is what you call poise. Anyway, naturally Ted looked up and saw me and was drinking me in until a tray of croquettes bumped me in the back and I unexpectedly sat down in Jerry's lap.

"Get out of my plate!" Jerry howled. "My, but you're annoying me to-night, Maudie."

"Good heavens, Maud," Sylvia said, and I could hear Ted asking Jane in an undertone who I was.

"That's Maud, Sylvia's younger sister," Jane said in a bored voice; "she's just filling in — she's only a kid — still going to school."

Well, I just smiled to myself as I saw how Jane was quickly digging my grave so I wouldn't be any dangerous competition. If she had known my real motive, she probably would have concentrated on cutting Sylvia's throat, as being a husband for Sylvia is a much more serious thing for a girl to have happen to a man than being my passion.

I talked very charmingly to Davy while he guzzled his croquette, so that I was naturally not surprised when Ted leaned across the table when the music started and said:

"I must dance with the little sister. I like youth."

I gave him a suspicious look.

"What do you know about it?" I asked, looking at each part of his face separately, which seems to upset people. Davy gave a loud laugh.

"Now don't be mean," Ted said, coming around to my chair, "you mightn't look your best either, if you'd just spent six hours on a day train."

"I always look my best," I said. "A girl can't afford not to."

"Then you just didn't want to dance with me, I'll bet," he said, folding me to him in a way that made me forget for a minute how badly Sylvia needed a husband. "I never saw a more unfriendly expression than that one of yours." He did some queer little steps to one side and gazed down at me from one heel.

"I'm not keen about duty dances," I said. "I can't get interested — it's just too bad."

That of course inflamed him to the point of making me his life work that evening, which was my reason for using it, for I felt that I could build Sylvia up better if she could come into the conversation naturally as our friendship grew.

Davy cut in then, still chortling over my clever come-back to Ted. Davy's appreciation is very touching. Then Jerry cut in and gave me an amused smile and then Ted cut back.

"This time it's all to the good," he said, "and I don't want to hear any more about duty dances. I love you for yourself."

"Well, you're one of the few that do," I said, with a sigh, inwardly apologizing to myself; "most men think I'm a good way to get them one step closer to Sylvia and so I get a big rush."

"You're breaking my heart," Ted said, "and I don't believe you, anyway. You've got the stuff all right, or I'm momentarily insane."

"That might be," I agreed pleasantly. "You don't know Sylvia very well either, do you? I mean you haven't heard much about her reputation or anything, I suppose."

Ted looked interested.

"Why, no," he said, "I wish you'd tip me off. I didn't know she was one of these girls with a past."

"She can't help it," I said, low and melancholy. "It's just that she has millions of desperate heavy beaux and all her affairs are so tragic."

The music stopped just then and I started immediately for our table, never looking back at him. But in that last moment I knew by the look in his eye that I had made the supreme sacrifice. He was Sylvia's. I felt a little bitter about it, just for the moment.

The next afternoon was Saturday, however, and when Davy and Chi and Bob Lindsay came rattling around in the model-T with Pauline to get me to go to the movies, which was a marvellous one called "Her Hour of Passion", and then to get sprill sundaes at Wagner's, where you get the third one free if you can eat it, after which we all sat in the car in front of our house, singing some song which started, "Nobody loves a Man with a Wig or a Girl with a Wooden Leg", — well, I just thought to myself, who wants love when they are having such a swell time?

Jerry was lying on our sofa, reading the *Saturday Evening Post* as usual, when I finally went in, Father having called rather unsympathetically out of his window when we all started singing alto. Alas, Father is not musical.

"Listen," Jerry said, "you may look like a child, but you have the mind of a politician. Do you know what happened here this afternoon?"

"What?" I said, not specially caring.

"Ted Felton was here," Jerry said accusingly, "and he took Sylvia to the theater. Just how do you explain that?"

I stared at him in disgust.

"When I was explaining every one of my thoughts to you last Wednesday," I said, "were you dead or just unconscious? What do you mean, how do I explain that?"

"Maudie," Jerry said, "this is serious. What did you say to Ted Felton, who is this year's biggest news around women, that gets him here waving theater tickets just about when Sylvia wakes up from having met him. I give Sylvia high marks all right, but this romance looks too quick to be on the level. You told that guy something."

"Don't be dull," I said. "After all, what is a girl going to do when she's nineteen and single?"

"That's just the point," Jerry said. "I don't think she did anything. But you did. What I want to know is, what was it?"

"And what I want to know is, is this a home or a police station?" I said, turning on the phonograph. "You ought to be able to figure out what would intrigue a man. You're a man — or are you?"

I was just beginning to sway gently to some divine music, but the next thing I knew Jerry, the big bully, had reached up and grabbed me by the back of my neck and pushed my head down so I fell over his lap, where he was spanking me with the *Saturday Evening Post*. I never in my life was so mad. And just at that minute the door opened and in walked Sylvia, looking as sophisticated as a divorcée and Ted towering behind her.

I kicked and bit Jerry's knee until he finally let me roll off onto the floor, where I sat with my back to everybody, trying to pin back my hair which was all mussed, and my disposition, too.

"Good heavens, Maud," Sylvia said in that annoyed tone. "What are you doing?"

"What is the wife-beater doing, you mean," Ted said, hitting Jerry on the back. "Want me to throw him out, Maudie?"

"I wish you'd kill him," I said, not turning around. "Some kind of a lingering death."

"Okay," Ted said, and he was just about to fall on Jerry when Sylvia stopped him.

"Don't be childish," she said. "Maudie, go tell

126

"Good heavens, Maud," Sylvia said in that annoyed tone. "What are you doing?"

Nora Ted's staying for supper, will you? What time did you say we had to leave to-night, Jerry? It's the dance in Wilmington," she explained to Ted.

"Nine-fifteen," Jerry said. "It'll take us an hour and a half at least. I'll be here around nine. Good-by, infant," he walked over and twisted my hair; "now you're one of those lucky girls that's been on my lap."

Well, after that I thought to myself, why live? Besides not liking to be taken lightly in front of an attractive man like Ted — even though I was trying to make him Sylvia's — a person has to have some self-respect. Sylvia went up to change her clothes after Jerry left, and Ted sat down in Father's chair by the wood basket.

"He's a ten-minute egg," he said casually. "Somebody ought to kick him in the — that is, wring his neck for him. You must be pretty mad."

"No," I said, looking up at him pensively. "I'm just feeling sort of frustrated."

I stared into the fire. Ted nodded respectfully.

"I see," he said, "I feel that way sometimes. When it happens, I'm in terrible shape."

"You know," I said, "in some movie I saw, there was a very disillusioned man who when the movie ended was looking out at some waves and saying in a low sad voice: 'A man and a woman can never

129

be friends.' I thought to myself how dumb, but now I'm beginning to wonder if I wasn't pretty immature at the time. That was way back in February."

"Life is like that," Ted said, getting out a cigarette. "Just about the time you think you got it all doped out, it turns around and plays you for a fish."

"Yes, life is like that," I sighed, thinking how pleasant it was to be sitting there thinking deep thoughts without somebody jumping on you and kicking you around. "Some days I'm sort of tired of this world."

Ted tipped his head back and blew smoke at the ceiling.

"Do you ever think about marriage?" he said. "Some of those seem to go rather well."

I felt very soothed inside. It's nice, having people ask your opinion about things.

"Sure I think about marriage," I said; "what able-bodied girl doesn't?"

Ted coughed very loud as if something caught in his throat.

"But every girl has a dream man," I went on sadly, "and dreams never come true."

"Just what sort of man does appeal to women?" he asked. "I've always wondered what got over with them."

"Well, a girl wants a knight with a lot of feathers," I said, pushing back the piece of my hair that kept falling in my eye. "I mean, she'd rather have him thrilling and dashing and maybe even cruel — than just sweet and sympathetic."

"Jerry's your dish, then," Ted said. "He was cruel."

I looked at him with dignity.

"Jerry was insulting," I said. "It would have been different if he had broken my leg, for instance."

"I get you," Ted said, "but I know fellows like you described — I mean the dashing, reckless type — and they're pretty bum husbands on the whole. How do you account for that?"

I got up on account of my foot being asleep and hopped around while thinking.

"They probably had flits for wives," I said, "so I suppose they went and got some mistresses, didn't they?"

"Maudie!" Ted said, scratching his head in an embarrassed way, "I didn't say — "

"If more wives would act like mistresses," I went on casually, "there would be fewer mistresses."

Ted pointed his cigarette at me.

"I didn't know any sixteen-year-old girl could possibly have that much wisdom."

"I don't suppose they have," I said regretfully. "That came out of that movie I was telling you about. How did you know I was sixteen?"

"Sylvia told me," he said, and can you believe it, that was absolutely the first moment I remembered about Sylvia. I could have kicked myself when I realized how I might have been putting the wings on her all this time instead of us having one conversation after another on other subjects. However, a person has to be themselves every so often, and when Sylvia came in a few minutes later, in one of these slinking lace dresses with a swirl of ruffles around her feet, I figured that I could rest back for the evening and she could go under her own steam.

There was a certain coolness between me and Jerry the next few days, but as Ted was always in our library, too, I was spared the unpleasantness of having to speak to him much. I got in some good work on Sylvia's romance, for one night I mentioned to Ted that I thought Sylvia was losing that haunted look she'd had after her lover who was in the Diplomatic Corps committed suicide when she turned him down; and then later on in the week, when Father sent me to get the mail and there were about forty letters, it being the first of the month, Ted was sitting on our porch railing when I got back and I simply waved them and said, "All for

132

Sylvia" in a casual way. You could see Ted looked impressed.

But the climax came one night when Ted brought Sylvia home from a dance, and they sat in the car in the drive for quite a while, laughing and talking. I sat huddled up at my window until Sylvia got out and I heard her say, "To-morrow night around nine. I'll know for sure by then, I promise you," and he said, "You're so good to me", and they both went into the vestibule. As I gazed out the window, I felt a surge of triumph sweep over me, and I felt a little sad too.

Love is a funny thing, though, and I wasn't taking any premature curtain calls yet, until he had actually come at nine the next night, like Sylvia said, and they were actually engaged. I literally slaved all day to get the house looking like the kind of a house a man would like to marry into, and around lunch I suggested to Mother that she and Father simply must see "Her Hour of Passion" as it was really a magnificent drama and it was closing that night. As I said that, there was a sound like a snort in the doorway and there was Jerry.

"Why, Jerry," Mother said, "I didn't expect you for lunch or I should have bought more chops. Shall Nora cook you some eggs?"

"No, thanks, Mrs. Mason," Jerry said, sitting

133

down in the place beside me, "I ate at the club. Are you really going to see that lousy — ouch!"

I had kicked him silently on the ankle. Mother has a secret passion for movies in spite of her years but she is very easily discouraged.

"Mother and Father are going to see this marvellous movie which everybody is just raving about," I said, kicking Jerry again. "It has the most supreme moral." The moral is that if you lead a wild life of sin like this girl in the movie, your husband will end by divorcing you and marrying some wicked demi-mondaine who will wreck his life.

"What's the big idea sending the family out among the wild oats?" Jerry said, after Mother had gone. "My ankle is as big as a duck egg, just in case you're interested."

"I'm not," I said, reaching for another cake; "you keep your talons off my affairs, will you, Jerry Hart? If this falls apart, it will just be your fault."

"Nix," Jerry said, "you can't blame your troubles on me this time. You haven't spoken to me for a week."

"You may not be a trouble-maker," I said haughtily, "but you're a constant source of irritation. This is going to be an absolutely crucial night, and I need coöperation, or else you better just shut up."

"Check," Jerry said, also reaching for a cake. "In my own small way I'm here to help. What's up?"

"Sylvia and Ted are getting engaged here at nine o'clock to-night," I said dramatically.

Jerry laid down his cake very carefully and looked at me with a serious look.

"What makes you think so?" he said.

"I don't think. I know," I said, and I told him how I had heard Sylvia tell Ted "to-night at nine" and how he had said, "You're so good to me," and how they had stood so long in the vestibule.

"You know how he's been here practically constantly all the time this week," I said, "and didn't he bring Sylvia home from three dances? And when I thought he might be slipping," I finished modestly, "I would tell him things."

"I'll bet you did," Jerry said in a grim voice. "Yes, it sounds like a natural. You are some little fixer."

"Oh, I don't know," I said, although I was feeling pretty proud of myself, "something might happen even now, especially if you get Father and Mother to stay home and read this evening. Love needs a lot of privacy, especially in the early stages."

Jerry went back to the office just after that and around four Sylvia came home from where she had been taking the new Junior League girls through the jail. Then the telephone rang and it was for her and she came out in a minute to shut the door of the telephone room so I couldn't hear her conversation. I smiled understandingly to myself as I got a couple of bananas in the pantry. Suspense always makes me hungry.

I had heard Sylvia tell Mother that morning she was going over to Dora's for supper because they had to pay the Junior League Dinner-Dance bills, and so when I heard the front door close after a while, I knew I was alone. Father telephoned to say he and Mother would stay in town for dinner, so they actually were going to the movies, and no one would muss up the library after I got it fixed. I changed half the electric-light bulbs for the kind that aren't only half as bright, and I pushed the sofa around with its back to the door, and I got out all the old records that Sylvia loves and laid them on the stool by the phonograph. Then I threw away all the old newspapers that Father is always saving and I straightened up his desk, which was covered with little piles of bills with a check on each bill. I put all the checks in one cubbyhole in his desk and all the bills in the drawer where he keeps all the old bills. though why I can't imagine.

Mother had left a lot of little lists on the piano, which I threw in the fire, and there was a letter from the Gas Company for some man named John Biggs, which the postman had left at our house by mistake, and I threw that in the fire too. When I got done, it was certainly a different-looking library, and I felt rather pleased with it all.

At half-past eight, though, I began to get worried. Sylvia hadn't come home, and I was afraid Ted would get there first. It got to be quarter of nine and then five minutes of, and at nine I was wildly walking the floor. When the doorbell rang at ten after, it just about threw me into a swoon. I heard Nora let Ted in, and I heard him go into the library where if ever Sylvia should have been sitting in the glow of the firelight that I had lit myself, that was the time. It got to be quarter after nine and then twenty after, and I decided I would have to go down or he would leave before Sylvia got there. Imagine paying the Junior League's bills when you could be getting engaged!

"Hello!" Ted said, jumping up as I went into the library, "this is great! This is simply great! Sit down," and he led the way to the sofa I had fixed for him and Sylvia.

"I can't imagine where Sylvia is," I said, "she said she was going over to Dora's — "

"Never mind," Ted said, looking at me with

that dominant smile that made me go weak in the knees, while thinking how I would enjoy suffering for his sake, "you and I have lots to talk about."

"Yes," I said, with a sweet but sisterly smile, "and so have you and Sylvia, I guess," and I did my best to hold the fort for her by telling him a lot about the wonderful domestic side of her nature, which I made up as I went along, but the waiting or something had put Ted in a most unloverlike mood, as I found out when I finally had to stop and come up for air.

"You're right," he said, putting on a very serious expression, "Sylvia has the stuff — or I'm no judge of horseflesh." The devastating thing about this remark was that there are times when Sylvia does look faintly like a horse.

I was still wondering if I could of possibly heard right, when there was a click and the door opened, and there was Sylvia, looking very happy and misty-eyed and her hair all mussed, and Jerry looking stern and stubborn and his ears were red.

"Sorry, Maudie darling," Sylvia said, in a voice that I have literally never heard her use to me before — a sort of a soft, shaking voice, "but it's Jerry and I that are engaged." Then she leaned over the back of the sofa and hugged me and said in my ear, "Thank you, dearie", which didn't make sense to me then.

"It's all right this time," Jerry said, glaring at me, "but after this you lay off this Cupid stuff or I'll have to spank you again. I almost had heart failure." Then they went into Father's study.

I just stared dumbly at the door which they had shut after them and my emotions felt as though they had been drawn through the keyhole. Ted laughed and not a bit in the bitter way you'd expect from a broken-hearted lover, and then we had the most staggering conversation.

"I could see she was in love with him the night I met her," Ted said. "The way she looked at him when he cut in and the way she talked to me about him. He was in love with her, too, but Jerry is such a caboose when it comes to catching on with women. Congratulations on knocking the barnacles off him. How'd you do it?"

"You did it," I said, realizing suddenly what Sylvia had meant by thanking me, "only I picked you for Sylvia's husband."

"Me?" Ted blinked. "I think she is a charming, delightful and most attractive girl, and stunning to look at, and I think it's terrible what you've been doing to her reputation. But — why, in heaven's name, did you pick on me?"

Well, I reminded him of how he'd been taking Sylvia to the theater and haunting the house.

"Just a lonely stranger in a strange land," he said. "I craved company."

"But you acted awful sort of lovery in the car last night," I protested. "And I heard you say to Sylvia in the most soulful tones, 'You're so good to me.'"

"Oh, that," Ted laughed in an embarrassed way. "Well, you see, Maudie — well, you see — the truth is — I thought I might strike a couple of your father's friends in Boston for a policy — I sell life insurance — and Sylvia had just promised to get him to write letters for me."

And I'd actually been wishing Ted could be my knight! Alas, there aren't any really romantic men any more.

VI

SURPRISE ENDING

WITH Sylvia safely out of the way, I was able once more to give a little serious thought to my own life, which it certainly needed at this point, what with rehearsals starting for a play I was the leading lady in and me loathing the hose-out they'd picked for hero. And then, on top of that, Davy got mulish and said he wouldn't be in it at all.

"All I got to say is," he kept saying sourly, "I know one guy you won't see in those blue underdrawers."

"Don't be loathsome, Davy," Mary said, dumping down her ping-pong set. "Those are tights. Don't you see, all this happens somewhere in the

Middle Ages at some tavern, and you'll look funny wearing those hockey pants."

"No, I won't," Davy said, putting his feet up on the piano bench, "because I'm not going to be in the lousy play — heh! heh!"

"You would if your mother was home," Pauline said, pushing off his feet and opening up the bench. "She'd make you. Who took all the new music out of here? Darn it, I haven't even played it yet."

"Bill just borrowed it," Mary said apologetically; "Miss McCord said he had to carry real music in the tavern scene where he is the wandering minstrel. She says everything has to be true to life, even little details like Bill's music."

"Well, I hope he don't lose it," Pauline said, "because it's got Rudy Vallee's picture all over the front, the divine man."

Bob Lindsay came in and threw his cap across the room at Davy.

"You big pansy," he said, winding his arm around Davy's throat, "welching on the gang like you're doing. Now you just tool over to the try-outs before I squeeze your neck, you big droop."

"Nobody sucks me in to act in any play," Davy gasped, "for a looloo with ideas in her head like this looloo. Lay off, will you?"

"You make me sick," Bob said, gradually stran-

142

gling Davy, "Who wants to be in any play? Only we gotta, on account of this dame that wrote it is somebody Mrs. Garrison knows."

"Well, what of it?" Davy said. Men have no social sense.

"I suppose you are not aware that Mrs. Garrison is the social leader of this town," I said witheringly, "and our mothers are all making us go in it so she won't get mad."

"If she's such a big shot in society, why'd she have a droop like Alfred for her son then?" Davy asked, giving a Bronx cheer for Alfred.

"It's what they call heredity," Bill Brandt said from the dining room, where he was screwing on the ping-pong net, "if anybody wants to know."

"We don't," Mary said. She's Bill's sister and so doesn't have a very high opinion of his intelligence. "What we want to know is how to keep Alfred from hogging the show. Go on and be villain, Davy. It isn't fair for you to back out. Come on, Bob, we're playing Pauly and Bill. Bring the whosis, will you?"

"Maudie," Davy said, with a pleading expression, trying to find his tie, "you know it isn't any big shot of fun for me to take on this play, see what I mean — see? I mean, is it a good play?"

"It's swish," I said.

"Yeah," Davy said enthusiastically, "and even

143

if it was good, I wouldn't like it. You know I'd be a sad job out there on a stage, Maudie."

"Well," I said, staring out the window, "I guess this is my big frustration. Just the very thought of kissing Alfred Garrison again gives me the creeps."

"What do you mean!" Davy said, leaping up. "What do you mean, kissing Alfred Garrison again. You didn't say you were the heroine."

"Yes, of course I'm the heroine. I mean, yes, I'm the heroine," I said. "Why?"

"Why? Well, gosh, why didn't you say so? Nobody wants this big mutt Garrison soaking up space around you, Maudie. You don't mean to say he kisses you, the pud."

"Well, somebody has to," I said pathetically, "and Miss McCord decided on him for hero on account of the way his hair grows down the side of his face and he looks so swell in feathers."

"Now, Maudie," Davy said, collapsing on the piano keys, "you don't mean to sit there and tell me this guy comes walking over and kissing you with nothing on but feathers?"

"On his hat," I explained patiently. "Bob Lindsay tried out for hero and his hat fell off every few minutes, and then she tried Bill — "

"And who else?" Davy said bitterly. "Quite a little party you had, it looks like, with a line form-

144

ing down the sidewalk. I suppose this is a perfectly nice play, oh, yes?"

"Pure to a fault," I said haughtily. "Only a person with your kind of a mind would think of lines forming down sidewalks. They didn't try out the kissing part, dumb-bell. Nobody needs to try out on an act of nature. It's the place where Ramon says, 'Is this the daughter of my gracious liege? Is this the fair Antigone?' and I say, 'Even so, my lord,' and then over behind the rocks Rodolfo says, 'Ha! ha! ha!' very loud and scornful."

"Who's Rodolfo?" Davy said, brightening. "I like that guy."

"Why, he's the villain," I said hopefully. "You'd make a supreme villain, Davy. I'd feel so much — safer." I shrank back timidly. Davy glowered.

"No, but, Maudie," he said, "when this pud kisses you, do you just have to stand there and take it? In the story, I mean."

"No," I said, "I kiss him."

Davy paled.

"Not — not on the smush, Maudie?"

I looked out the window over at some curtains flapping out a window across the street.

"You see," I said dreamily, "I'm supposed to have a sort of mad passion for Ramon."

Well, with one thing and another, I wasn't surprised to see Davy's model-T leaning up against the curb in front of the Community House when Bob Lindsay and I got there the next afternoon. Bob was my father in the play and I was helping him bring in the arms of his throne, because Miss McCord believes in rehearsing with the properties, so that you will gradually absorb them into your being.

"You must of put the bee on Davy," Bob said, idly blowing the model-T's horn as we passed. "How'd you work it, bright girl?"

"I didn't," I said, stumbling over the galosh scraper by the front door. "I just appealed to his honor. I bet you don't know that part where you inflame the army to rush out and rescue me. I sounded like a perfect dud the way you plodded through my eulogy yesterday."

"I couldn't help it," Bob said, pushing open the door with his back, "McCord kept switching the lights on me and I kept thinking they had cut out the rest of my speech. It's a lousy speech, anyway. 'Now gather here, ye chieftains bold, Ye lancers and dragoons, The victor here shall share my throne, My spoils and my — "

"Spittoons," guffawed a voice above us and there was Davy, hanging over the railing, dripping a little ice water on us from a paper cup.

"I'm shy," he said, as we tore upstairs. "I don't

146

know this job in here running things. You take me in, Maudie."

Everybody was milling around in a very unco-operative way in the Assembly Room where the stage is. Miss McCord was working over the wandering minstrels and trying to get Bill Brandt to smile while he sang, while Alfred Garrison sat at a little table, staring moodily off into the fuse box, which at that point was meant to be the coast of Spain. I introduced Davy to Miss McCord, who is one of these people with a bulging forehead and slightly pop-eyes and an ingrowing smile which when she doesn't smile just looks like a cavity in her face. She was very pleased, especially as Davy had a rather fierce expression on his face.

"My Rodolfo at last," she said, coyly patting his shoulder. "How very fortunate!"

Behind me I heard Alfred Garrison snort. I was really afraid to look at Davy.

"Now will every one take his or her place," Miss McCord said, "and you, Daniel, read the parts marked 'Rodolfo.' " And she put the leaflet into Davy's limp hand.

"Now let us get into the spirit of the play," Miss McCord went on. "The scene opens on the market-place of the city of Cordova at the height of the fiesta. Revellers throng the streets in an orgy of feasting and celebration. Mr. Chapman's Bible

147

Class has very kindly consented to act as the revellers. As the curtain rises, the king and queen enter to mingle with the throng. All quiet now. Robert and Estelle!"

" 'Slucky this is the Middle Ages," Bob said, gripping Estelle by the elbow. "Nowadays somebody would drop a bomb on me, circulating around without my plain-clothes man."

"Curtain!" rang out Miss McCord.

Bob and Estelle rushed in and stood huddled together in the middle of the stage.

"Ah, what a scene of mirth is this, What revelry and song, Come let us cast dull care behind, And mingle with the throng," said Bob in a dead voice.

"Mingle! Mingle!" called Miss McCord. "A little life, a little feeling of abandon. Mingle!"

"What with?" Bob demanded. "Estelle and I can't buddy up with thin air."

"Use your imagination," said Miss McCord; "imagine crowds and revellers elbowing you on every side."

"I feel like a drip," Bob muttered, walking around in a circle.

"My liege, my heart is weighed with fears, I feel impending grief," said Estelle hollowly. Estelle is really a wonderful actress. "Who are these strangers in the crowd? Behold yon skulking thief!"

148

"Just like a woman," Davy said to me in the wings, where he was squinting at the part, "getting the heebie-jeebies the first time the king goes out on a bust."

"Enter Rodolfo!" Miss McCord said in a loud voice.

"That isn't the heebie-jeebies," I said to Davy, "that's woman's intuition. This is a rather deep play, once you get into it."

"To me," Davy said, "this is going to be just one long living death."

"Enter Rodolfo!" Miss McCord shouted in a refined though indignant way. "Where *are* you, Daniel? Every one must watch his or her cue."

Davy stumbled out on the stage, wildly looking for his part. Alfred gave a sort of a snort over in the other wings, and I saw Davy's face jell into a horrible expression of savage loathing.

"Excellent!" said Miss McCord gaily. "Excellent! I have my Rodolfo!"

But when the kissing scene came, Davy got a little out of hand. He and his ruffians are holding me captive in a cave on the coast of Spain, and Alfred comes in and slews all the ruffians and then confronts Davy. Davy was still reading off the book and looking worried, not knowing what was coming.

"Crude mountebank, your end is near," Alfred

said, with a snort, leering at Davy. "Your day of glory done. Release this maiden ere I swell the carnage I've begun."

"What ransom do you offer?" Davy said in a wooden voice, peering at the book.

"Ransom! Ha! My arm shall serve," Alfred said, edging up to where Davy seemed to have taken root.

"Oh, Ramon, quell his fiery nerve," I moaned at Alfred, while pinching Davy in the kneecap. "Act, lemon, act!" I whispered frantically, but Davy just stood there scowling bewilderedly.

'That for him," Alfred said, snapping his fingers, "and that and that," and he slapped Davy twice in the face, while a terrible silence swept over the cast. Then Alfred drew me to his nauseating embrace and was just kissing me in that loud triumphant way that makes any subtle woman shudder when what should happen but Davy hit him on the ear.

"No! no! no!" Miss McCord cried wildly, " 'Rodolfo is felled by the blow, he shudders and is still.' "

"If anybody thinks," Davy said loudly, "tha I'm going to stand up here and let this blemish pusl me around in front of five hundred people — "

"Oh, act the play," Bill said disgustedly. "It's only a play."

SURPRISE ENDING

"Try to grasp the effect of this surprise ending, Daniel," Miss McCord argued. "Just as the audience gives up hope — enter Ramon to the rescue!"

Well, I just thought to myself, thinking that ending would surprise anybody was just what a person would think who kept calling Davy Daniel.

"Surprise?" said Bob in sarcastic tones, over by the door.

"I beg your pardon?" Miss McCord said. "Now attention, everybody. We'll take the play over again from the beginning."

It was plain to see that Davy was under a terrible strain, but what could you expect from a fiery nature like him? I began to wish I had never suggested him going in the play.

When the rehearsal was over, I was the last person to get my things, so I turned out the Assembly Room light and shut the fuse box. Miss McCord went into the Board Room to see Miss Lola Le Roy from the society column of the *Chronicle*, and I started down the stairs in the dark, carrying my sheaf of lilies and my geometry book and Bill Brandt's yo-yo which he left in the tavern scene. I was going very carefully, because the stairs go round and round, and if you get on the inside you are just as apt to skid off six or eight steps and maybe hurt yourself or drop something. Just as

I went around the last curve, something jumped out at me with a deep groan and I simply fell apart with fright. I sat down on the step so hard that the lilies shot out the front door, and the yo-yo went trickling down the hall. Then a cold damp hand closed around one side of my neck, which nearly threw me into a swoon, until I heard a sort of a snort very near me and my eyes narrowed in the darkness.

"Keep your talons off me, Alfred Garrison," I said in a calm voice; "I have trouble enough in my life without you."

I heard the light click on and there was Alfred laughing his internal laugh so hard he simply hung over and shook.

"Oh, my gosh, you were funny," he said, reaching out and slapping my ankle. "I never heard anybody sit down so hard."

I kicked off his hand and stood up, realizing with rage that he was right, as I felt all bruised on the back of my lap. I never was so mad in all my life, for if there is anything less complimentary than a person mentioning the way you sat down and how hard and all, I should like to know what it is. I drew myself up and started to walk coldly down the stairs, when Alfred leaned his hand on the railing and blocked my way, laughing his horrible silent laugh.

"Would you mind letting me get by?" I said, feeling like going into a tantrum if it weren't for my dignity.

"Oh, how polite! Oh, my! how polite!" Alfred jeered.

"Yes," I said, "anybody knows it is safer to act polite to idiots and lunatics."

"Oh, really?" Alfred said, "Because they might hurt little girls?" But it takes more than Alfred to catch up to my naturally quick mind.

"No," I said, edging up closer to him, "because it throws them off their guard," and I pulled up my knee, unexpectedly, hitting him in the stomach, after which he doubled up with a grunt and I nearly fell downstairs getting out the door. In a minute I heard him tearing after me. Well, I thought what with a person leaping out of dark corners and blocking staircases, I would do better to get invisible as quick as possible, so I ducked around the corner of the Assembly Building and dived over the side of the first car I saw. I just lay there with my head on the brake and my feet on the seat until I heard Alfred go by. Then I looked up and there, sitting behind the wheel, was Davy, and it turned out to be his car.

"Bats?" he asked, jerking his head back the way Alfred ran.

"Bats," I said.

153

There was a long silence.

"You got your heel on my lung," Davy said, after a while. I began to snake myself around until my feet fell on the floor and I could climb up.

"I musta been waiting here about one hour," Davy said, "up to when you dropped in. Did you get that, Maudie? Dropped in."

"You're too stimulating, Davy," I said, feeling sure I owed him something, "specially when I think about Alfred."

"What's the idea thinking about him for?" Davy almost shouted.

I shuddered.

"I lie awake nights thinking about his mouth."

"What the hi! thinking about his mouth?" Davy sounded exasperated.

"When he kisses me," I brooded, "it's like being kissed by a clam. A wet clam."

Each day there was more and more about us in the paper and also long write-ups about Miss McCord's other plays and what howling successes they always were and what an uplifting influence in the lives of the young people of Buffalo, Grand Rapids, Salt Lake City and other places. Everybody bought tickets and Miss McCord issued quite a few fight talks about how the city was thundering in applause of a new and pioneer experiment, which we must consider a challenge to our best efforts. I had an idle suspicion that the city was really thundering in applause of Mrs. Garrison, each person trying to thunder the loudest so she would look over and say, "Ah, there is a kindred soul," because most everybody would give their right eye to be Mrs. Garrison's kindred soul. Everything she gets interested in right away becomes the life work of so many people, I thought to myself.

The night before the play the evening paper said that Mrs. Garrison would have as her guest Mr. George Dean Layton, noted dramatic critic, which just about threw everybody into a swivet. I even felt a little shaky myself, in spite of my cool exterior. We were having the last rehearsal that night, and as I walked in the door, Miss McCord was reading about Mr. Layton to the cast.

"Come on," Bob muttered in my ear. "Get in on the glad news. McCord's going pro on us."

"Will every one take his or her place for the last act," Miss McCord said, "the others may sit down. Now please let us get this last act right. Daniel — "

"Oh, scum," Davy inhaled back of me.

" — must remember that in this scene he is the menace upon which the surprise ending hinges, but only a menace. Now let us begin."

I sat down on one of the bags of doubloons and

Davy stood beside me, with his hand resting wood-enly on my shoulder. We looked just like an old daguerreotype, ready to burst into "Old Black Joe." I could see that Davy's heart was not in it.

"Crude mountebank, your end is near," Alfred said, bounding through the door of the cave, "Your day of glory done, Release this maiden ere I swell, The carnage I've begun."

"What ransom do you offer?" Davy asked, as one stockbroker to another, after the crash.

"With venom, with venom," Miss McCord said impatiently, making futile gestures with her elbows.

It was no use, though. As a mere menace, Davy was a flop, he being naturally a man of action, and I shuddered to think how warped his personality was probably getting. Each time we would do it I would wind myself around his knees, supposedly because my spirit was crushed and I was pleading for mercy, but really to keep him from sitting down and glowering or walking out on me with something else on his mind. And each time Alfred would push him over like a snow man, and each time I would choke over Alfred's kiss and Davy would give me a bitter look. It was terrible.

At dinner the next night Father and Mother and Sylvia thought it would be kind to talk a little about the play, considering it began in an hour.

156

"I do hope they'll be able to hear at the back," Mother said, giving me a sympathetic smile; "the acoustics of that room are so bad."

"Remember that time Admiral Byrd spoke there," Sylvia said, eating her third roll, thinking I didn't notice, "you couldn't tell what he was talking about."

"Didn't I read somewhere about him going to the South Pole?" I said, feeling very gone in my stomach. "That should have given you a clue."

"It's not a very successful place for entertainments," Mother went on. "It's really too wide and the stage is too high."

"Will you ever forget the time Georgie Barron backed off the edge in the children's orchestra concert," Sylvia said, chewing enthusiastically. "He turned a regular backflip. It was simply hysterical."

"What happened?" Father said.

"It was a scream," I said; "he broke his leg."

Bob stopped for me after dinner, because we had to assemble the throne. When we got to the Community House, people were already going in and there was music from the Boy Scout band, which we could hear coming out the open windows. I began to feel practically paralyzed with fright and Bob's teeth clicked together like castanets all through his nonchalant chatter. There was a policeman waving cars around the block and keeping little boys from sitting in the trees to see in the windows.

Inside the stage door you might think we had stepped into a bad dream. In the boys' dressing room the dragoons were putting on their tights with the door wide open, for one thing, while people's chauffeurs kept delivering pieces of scenery like fountains, and shrines, and grassy knolls right into the rooms where we girls were supposed to leave our clothes. Everywhere you went you met Miss McCord, with a wild expression on her face and things in her hand that I bet she didn't know were there, like a hammer and Rudy Vallee's picture and the janitor's pipe.

"Maudie," Pauline moaned out of the costume room, "I can't make this skirt hook."

"You ate those sundaes," Mary said, looking really wonderful with a comb in her hair.

"That was this morning," Pauline said, "and it don't take nine hours to digest three sundaes. Darn it, if I even swallow it'll drop off, Maudie."

"Hurry up," Bill said, banging open our door, "the house is nearly full and McCord is dying by inches up by the town pump. Gosh, Maudie, you look like the last rose of summer in that white sheet."

Some of my old fire returned within me.

158

*People's chauffeurs kept delivering pieces of
scenery right into the room where we girls
were supposed to leave our clothes.*

"Thanks," I said, looking at Bill's minstrel costume, "you look like the last rows of the balcony with that hat."

"Come on, you two," Bob called in over Bill's ear, "Davy's going into a decline."

"This sure is stimulating," Pauline said, "hearing about the morale everywhere. I look like a poached egg in this costume. Come on, Maudie. If you were dead, you couldn't look prettier."

Davy was roaming around the stage, looking like the Depression in person.

"All right, all right," he said before any one had said a word, "I feel like a weezer in these curls. I bet this is going to be some play."

"You should know, wise guy," Bob said; "you're the menace. Woof! Woof!"

"Be quiet!" Miss McCord simply shot out of the monastery. "Do you realize that we have five hundred people on the other side of that curtain? Take your places at once."

I peeped around the curtain from the wings where I was meant to stand. There was Mrs. Garrison with a man with an unhappy face, who I supposed was Mr. Layton. I saw Mother and Father and Sylvia and Arthur Dear, one of Sylvia's standbys, sitting in the fifth row, telling everybody that I'd never acted before and they hadn't the vaguest idea what I'd be like. How symbolic that is, I thought dreamily. Then the curtain went up and there was Mr. Chapman's Bible Class milling around.

My own entrance was pretty good. I rush in carrying my lilies and throw myself on Estelle and say:

"I fly! I fly! I am pursued. My heart grows faint with dread. Three times he passed me in the throng. 'Twere better I were dead." Why I should notice one person passing me with the whole Bible Class everywhere, I didn't quite see, but it didn't matter. It went very well until the place where I meet Alfred and he says, "Is this the daughter of my gracious liege? Is this the fair Antigone?" Alfred all the time looking smug enough to make you shudder. I said, "Even so, my lord." And Alfred went and put his arm around me, which no king ought to allow, with him standing right there, looking at his own daughter. Davy forgot to say, "Ha! ha! ha!" and Miss McCord said it instead, loud and hysterical outside somewhere. It sounded pretty funny and some of the audience began to laugh.

When the curtain went down I was not very subtle. I didn't say anything, I just kicked Alfred.

"What's 'a matter, Antipathy?" he said. "Don't you love papa?"

"David, you are acting abominably," Miss

162

McCord was scolding. "Kindly remember that the entire surprise ending depends on you."

At the end of the tavern scene I have a lover's tryst with Alfred, the big octopus. He was supposed to lay a rose on my white palm while saying: "Love is a flower growing in my heart, I pluck it for thee before we part," only instead he laid a spitball in my hand.

That about love was the cue for the minstrels to come serenading in, which was a good thing, for in the noise and frolicking I quietly threw the spitball back at Alfred, only he ducked and it hit Davy in the back of his neck, where he was sitting at another tavern table. Davy turned around with a terrible expression, which was the first really good touch he'd given his part, and the first person he saw was Alfred, laughing his loathsome silent laugh.

Well, I could feel something brewing when Davy kidnapped me. Instead of me practically leading him off the stage, he dashed into where I was sitting alone at my table, grabbed me round my stomach till my tongue practically fell out, and dragged me away. The audience cheered, and it seemed to madden Davy, because he went right on dragging me around in an absent-minded way long after the curtain went down.

In the last act you could hear the audience

163

definitely getting into the spirit of the play. I sat on the bag of doubloons and looked at Davy, striding up and down with his arms folded and his curls behind his ears, and I thought what a supreme Ramon he would make.

Well, the curtain went up and you could hear Alfred killing people outside. Then he came dashing in, waving his sword and shouting:

"Crude mountebank, your end is near — "

"Yeah?" said Davy, "who says so?"

Alfred made a sound like a hiccup but he went on:

"Your day of glory done, Release this maiden ere I swell, The carnage I've begun."

"Are you losing weight?" Davy said, walking over and flipping off Alfred's hat, "or did you get a haircut?"

"What ransom do you offer?" Miss McCord whistled from the wings.

"I'm not asking for any ransom," Davy explained to Miss McCord, who nearly died of shock. "This is my girl and no guy can graft any time with her, especially any guy like this guy."

"Ransom? Ha! My arm shall serve!" Alfred said, in a loud voice.

"That's not an arm," Davy said, slapping it, while the audience began to giggle; "that's a fin."

"Oh, Ramon, quell his fiery nerve," Miss

McCord blew at me, where I had frozen to the doubloons. "Order! Order!"

"That's all right," Davy called over to Miss McCord, "we're just kicking Ramon around a little, the big drip." And he slapped Alfred on the cheek.

"That for him and that and that!" Ramon — I mean Alfred — yelled and hit Davy on the back so hard it's a wonder it didn't break his spine. The audience began stamping and cheering, and Davy simply fell on Alfred and they both hit the stage with a crash. Then Alfred began clawing Davy's curls and Davy began mashing Alfred's face and I figured I had better finesse this scene if I wanted to stay in one piece. All the cast were dashing around in a way that had nothing to do with the story, as half of them were supposed to be dead anyway, and Miss McCord was having hysterics by the fuse box and the audience was screaming and waving things, and the band was banging its drum to try to get people to sit down, and altogether you would never have suspected that this was supposed to be a lonely cave on the coast of Spain.

Suddenly the lights went out, which was probably Miss McCord fainting into the fuse box. When they went on again, Alfred had vanished and there I was in front of five hundred people, kissing Davy. His wig was gone and his coat was split down the back and his ruffle looked as though Alfred had chewed it, — and there was a terrible roar from the audience, which was all on its feet. I was just getting my startled gaze back into focus when the curtain fell with a crash.

Well, everybody rushed around and around Davy and me, wringing their hands and tearing their wigs.

"I'll say you sure tore your pants with this town," Bob said excitedly, pushing Davy and me apart. "What do you think you are? Cupid?"

"I wish you could see that grassy knoll out there," Mary said disgustedly, "Miss McCord sat right through the top. Honestly, Davy, it is too bad you haven't got just a few inhibitions!"

"After all this darn work!" Bill said, but Davy just gently kicked the bag of doubloons.

"That droop will never look the same," he said, seeming quite happy.

"No," Bill said, "and neither will you, after Mrs. Garrison and that angry mob swarm up here. Gosh, listen to those yells! I'll bet they wanta lynch you."

Miss McCord staggered out on the stage and flung out her arms in a wonderful gesture of despair.

"All of my work — all of my time and patience!" she began, only just then there was such a roar that nobody could hear themselves think and somebody in the audience caught the curtain rope and pulled up the curtain. There we stood like the Early Christians with every one howling around us, when all of a sudden we saw Mr. Layton coming up on the stage, leaving Mrs. Garrison looking as though she had had a stroke in the front row.

"That was priceless," he said, grasping Miss McCord's dangling hand; "but why didn't you warn us that this was intended as a satire on the theater? You are too subtle for us. The shock nearly killed us. Really, it was a fine job and this young man," he seized Davy, "has a real flair for comedy. I really envied you that last scene, especially with such a charming lady at stake." He smiled at me.

I put my hand on what some people are beginning to refer to as my bust and bowed.

CHAPTER VII

MEN ARE LIKE STREET CARS

AFTER the play nothing more interesting between me and Davy happened for a long time, because we were both cramming to get through our exams and then my family went down to the shore ahead of Davy's family. There I was, all set to go places and do things and no one to go with. It was too annoying. I now know what being a widow must feel like. Of course some of the rest of the crowd were there: Mary and Bill and Alix, who I hadn't hardly seen since last year, because she'd been away at boarding school.

"Well," I said one afternoon, pushing some of

Sylvia's candy, which luckily she is afraid to eat because of her complexion, toward Alix with a languid hand, "shall we start talking about boys or just let them come into the conversation naturally?"

"Maudie! How can you be so cynical?" Alix said, taking the last of my favorite kind out of the box in a shocked way.

"Cynical? Don't be dull," I said. "I just believe in looking at life as it is."

Alix burrowed idly among the spit-backs and found another piece of my favorite kind that I hadn't known was there. Alix better watch out. I say her figure is positively voluptuous because I'm her friend — if two equally popular girls can ever really be friends — but there are some flat-chested females in our crowd who are catty enough to call her just plain fat. It's only the girls, though, so Alix isn't worrying. She knows she could get a vote of confidence from the boys any time.

I always feel very satisfied, going around with Alix, because of the way we look so well together. Her black hair and black eyes make her look like one of these Russian princesses that they used to have in Russia, which is a perfect foil for my vivacious blond beauty. And the ironical thing about it all is that she has the superficial soul of a

169

dizzy blonde, whereas I, in spite of my silly though rather fetching yellow fluff, am by nature the thoughtful, intelligent type that wants to go beneath the surface of things.

"Well, I don't see why you think people have to always rave about boys," Alix said, "because it just happens to be a picnic I want to talk to you about."

"A hen picnic?" I asked coldly. I can think of nothing worse than a hen picnic.

"Good grief, no!" Alix said. "Can you imagine me having a hen picnic? Now really, Maudie. This is for — I — well, I've simply got to tell you, Maudie. I've got a new S. P."

I remained calm. This was not the first girlish confidence I had received from Alix about men. She is one of these intense people that has a new Secret Passion every little while.

"Why, I thought you were all wound up about the life guard," I said.

"Oh, him." Alix rubbed out the life guard with a tone that practically said he could drown any time, for all she cared. "No, this is the real thing. I've never felt like this before, ever. Just a smile or a kind word from Colin leaves me starry-eyed, and when he took my hand off the horn and went on holding it, gosh, was I disconnected and raving? *Mais oui*." Alix has that coy little habit of reaching over and leaning on the horn just as they are driving through a town, thus making all the citizens mad, until the boy has to take hold of her hand to get it off and then has to go on holding it to keep it off.

"Who is this Colin?" I said.

Well, even my heart was beating faster by the time Alix got through telling me about him. First of all, he was a lot older than these fuzzy-faced prep-school boys we'd been running around with. He'd be a sophomore in college when he went back to Penn in the fall. He was striking-looking but not too handsome, had a wonderful build, a new car and the cutest little fraternity pin with pearls in it. Alix was getting up a beach picnic out on the Point for the next night and she was asking me and the rest of the crowd, and Colin of course, and his kid brother Dick.

"They're both here for the golf tournament next week — just visiting. You can have Dick," she said, smiling a smug, superior, self-satisfied smile. "I give him to you."

"Thanks, big-hearted," I said, mentally wondering if Alix had any idea how my golf has improved. "What's wrong with him?"

"There you go being cynical again," Alix said. "Honestly, Maudie, he's darling — even if he is only sixteen. But I honies Colin; I saw him first."

171

Did I detect a slight note of anxiety in Alix's voice?

"No fear," I said reassuringly, while roughing up my back hair. "I'm not one to skunk a friend." But where men are concerned a girl has no friends, and I couldn't help wondering if Colin should just happen to prefer a blonde when he saw me, what could I do?

When I went over to Alix's the next evening, the first thing I saw was a moving mountain of blankets, ginger ale, frying pans and I don't know what all coming down the steps and in the center peering out a strange boy's face that I hadn't seen before, and from the looks of which I didn't care if I never saw it again. But guessing who it was, I smiled and a box of eggs dropped onto the side-walk.

"Hey, lame-brain!" came a hoarse yell from the porch. "Watch out what you're doing!"

I turned and there sitting on the porch steps was a handsome stranger nonchalantly eating a sandwich. I spotted the fraternity pin on his sweater right away and my pulse quickened because I knew it must be Colin.

"Were you addressing me?" I said with dignity.

The blah face in the blankets gave a gloating look and then hurried on to the car, as Colin came down the path wearing a sweater with some nu-

172

merals on it that you could see even though the sweater was modestly turned inside out. I became very busy picking up the eggs, which miraculously weren't only half of them broken.

"Hello," he said, bending down so he could peer into my face; "that was just one of my pet names for my kid brother."

"Oh," I said witheringly, handing him the eggs, which were really rather messy, "how stimulating."

"I wasn't trying to be stimulating, blond baby," Colin came back with an amused stare that went right through me, "but I can be;" and for the first time in perfect ages I felt myself blushing. Instead of embarrasing him, it was me that was really too embarrassed for words. A college education certainly does give a man poise.

"What are you insinuating, may I ask?" I said with hauteur, and just then Dick saved the situation by coming back from loading the stuff into the car. He stuck out his hand sort of bashfully, and I was about to shake it when Colin put what was left of the eggs in it.

"Meet the comic valentine," he said. This was too true to be funny, Dick peering out at the world through horn-rimmed glasses and being so sort of terribly clumsy with his hands and feet, which you can't exactly blame him for, though, as they are so big. But if he'd been Clark Gable

173

I couldn't have given him a more enticing smile.

"Stow the remains of those eggs in the car, kid," Colin quickly said in a lordly manner, not liking my smiling that way at Dick, I could see, "if possible without dropping them;" and Dick meekly did it. Stowed — not dropped — them, I mean. That should have warned me, I can see now. Sylvia would get an egg in the eye if she tried to boss me around like that.

Just then there was a screeching of brakes and some yells in front of a cloud of dust, and the rest of the crowd arrived, festooned all over Bill Brandt's flivver, with Bill singing loudly out of tune and Mary trying to throttle him. Mary is his sister and goes around with that tried expression that people usually have when their relatives show off. Alix came dashing languidly down the back steps calling, "When did you all get here?" and waving a necklace of hot dogs.

We all piled into the two cars, I calmly ignoring Colin's inviting smile and hopping lightly into the rumble with Dick, while Alix climbed in beside Colin like she owned him. Ha, ha, I thought, laughing silently.

Well, Ocean Avenue goes along for about a couple of miles beyond the last cottages and then stops at a sort of a dump where the dunes begin. Bill, who was ahead, pulled his flivver over to the side of the road when he got to the dump and every-body started to pile off.

"What's the idea?" Colin turned around to me, the way he'd been doing all the way out, as though Alix didn't exist. "Do we eat on the dump?" But I was too absorbed with Dick to even notice him.

"Oh, Colly, you're a howl!" Alix said, and laughed appreciatively in the way that a girl knows flatters a man to death. "We usually get out here and walk because Bill's car gets stuck in the sand."

"Well, I see tracks ahead, and where anybody else can go this wagon can," Colin said, shifting into second and stepping on the gas. We plowed along through maybe fifty yards of soft sand and then found ourselves out on a wide beach that was ab-solutely clean and smooth from having the ocean wash over it. It's too bad a person's soul couldn't be washed clean like that every little while, I thought. Colin stopped the car, and there was one of those rare moments that make you think you know what being in heaven must feel like. The top was back and the sea breeze blew through and through me and tasted clean and sort of salty in my mouth, and the waves came marching in and marching in just like some brave army, with fresh ones always ready to take the place of the ones which died on the shore. I just ached with happi-ness inside somewhere, the way I do when I'm dancing with some one I'm in love with and there's wonderful music.

Like all good things, it was over just about when I began appreciating it. The crowd caught up to us and swarmed all over the running boards and the mud guards.

"Hop on, gang," Colin invited unnecessarily, as they were all hopping on anyhow. "That was a cinch to get through, Bill; what were you afraid of?"

"Sure, you got through, coming down grade," Bill said; "but wait till you try to get over that little hump going back."

"Don't worry," Colin said, "I'm not. All I got to do is let some air out of my tires to get traction and I'll go through like a breeze." Bill looked sort of silly — he'd never thought of anything like that. Here, at last, was a Leo man that was a Leo man, I thought, as he started the car so emphatically that we practically lost a couple of the people hanging on the outside. We tore along on the dark, hard sand right at the edge of the water for miles. There was nothing around us but wind and water and sea and sky and the setting sun. Aside from being in a car, we were just like primitive man. It was too exhilarating and everybody started singing.

Finally we had to turn back on account of the beach getting bad, and when we came to a place where there were dunes, Colin turned the car up high on the beach, out of reach of the ocean, and we all piled out, as hungry as wolves. Us girls spread out the blankets and got the food organized while the men gathered a big pile of driftwood for the fire.

"Get up, darn it, you're all over everything!" Alix exclaimed, jabbing Colin, who had just collapsed after hauling up a tremendous log, with her toe, with a stricken look. "Darn it, you're leaning on the jelly sandwiches!"

"Can't I even put my elbow anywhere?" Colin said, looking around at me with an appealing expression. "Can't I, Maudie?"

"If you would just take your head off of the cheese dreams, everything would be daisy," I said, unconsciously silhouetted against the western sky and realizing that a person with my figure never has to worry about a sea breeze hitting them in the back.

"Look out!" Dick yelled, trying to open a bottle of warm ginger ale, while squinting for fear it would squirt in his eye, which it did. "Who wants this?"

"I do," I said sweetly, turning away from Colin and reaching out a paper cup, although really I think hot ginger ale is the horrors.

There is something fascinating about a drift-

177

wood fire at night, the way the flames are so many colors from the salt in the wood; and when everybody was about stuffed to the tonsils we collected the rather gruesome remains of what was left and threw them on the fire and piled on a lot more wood so as to have a real bonfire. Then we all sat around watching it, while digesting our dogs, sandwiches, ginger ale, eggs, cake, bacon, sand, cheese, etc., and thinking soulful thoughts. All except Alix, that is. Instead of watching the fire, she stared moodily out at the waves with that tense look she gets when trying to think. I just knew she was burning up the brain cells trying to win Colin back from me, he having been ignoring her all evening. And the hysterical part of it all was she couldn't even have the satisfaction of being mad at me for wolfing her man, because I had spurned his every advance. And of course Alix was too dumb to realize I was acting cold like that on the theory that a pot will come to a boil much quicker if you keep the lid on it.

Pretty soon we recovered from our gorge enough to sing, and Dick and I were enjoying it a lot, because he has a really quite nice voice except when it cracks, and although I'm not one to put the wings on myself, people have said I ought to go on the stage. Colin left Alix and came over beside me, as I was betting he would when he saw me seeming to have a good time with Dick. Brothers are even worse than sisters in wanting anything the other one has, and vice versa, and being willing to almost shed blood to get it.

"Quite the song birds, you two," he said.

"Yes," I said coldly, removing my hand which he had placed his over, much as I didn't want to.

"Maudie," he said irritably, after sitting beside me silently while I ignored him and went on singing 'Good Night, Sweetheart', with Dick, "be nice to me, won't you? I'm falling for you," and — oh, joy, oh, rapture! — what did he do but put his head in my lap! My fingers just itched to run through his nice crisp curls, and I realized I must do something quick if my maidenly modesty was to be preserved.

"What do I do now," I asked, playfully pouring a handful of sand in his ear, "jump up and clap my hands for joy?"

Well, it was Colin did the jumping up, trying to get the sand out of his ear, which he practically had to stand on his head to do, and for the time being he got all over being mushy with me. A girl can protect themself and still be at ease in any kind of a situation if she really wants to and has any sense — like looking cross-eyed at a man when he tries to pick you up, for instance.

Alix was about to have a fit and fall in it over the way she couldn't make any time with Colin, and it was very amusing to me to watch her trying to get his attention with all kinds of little womanly wiles, like tripping him up as he went by, carefully carrying the frying pan full of hot grease. Some of it slopped over on his hand, and I guess it burned him quite a lot, from the way he yelled. Anyhow, it seemed to infuriate him after just having got sand out of his ear, because just as we started to sing "Love's Old Sweet Song", he turned on Alix with a positively savage expression, and whether he actually knocked her down or not I couldn't be sure, but, anyway, the next minute she was screaming for help and he was sitting on top of her, rubbing her head in the sand. While her black bob was gradually turning gray — with the sand, that is — Bob Lindsay and Dick and Bill Brandt and the rest all fell to and dragged him off in a very dramatic way, and Alix started crying and carrying on like a mad woman and calling Colin a brute. A person can see through Alix like a plate-glass window. The flattery line she'd been using not working, she was trying something else. But men, they are all of them so terribly dumb they never see through anything, and the next minute Colin was practically groveling at her feet. It wasn't going to be so easy to take him away from

Oh, joy, oh, rapture! — what did he do but put his head in my lap!

her as I'd thought, and that made me want him all the more.

Dick came back and flopped down on the blanket beside me again, while I went on wondering what life would hold for me if I couldn't make Colin love me after all.

"Maudie," Dick said after a long silence, during which I'd been watching the fire die down and thinking how symbolical it was of Colin's interest in me, "you're in love."

"Isn't everybody?" I said airily, though somewhat startled, as you can well imagine, at the way he seemed to read my inmost thoughts.

"Yeah, but I'll bet I can prove who with," he said.

"I — I don't bet," I gulped, absolutely at a loss.

"Well, I'll be big-hearted and show you, anyway," he said. "It's a swell thing I heard somewhere. I say, 'I love you', first, see? Therefore I'm a lover. And all the world loves a lover, you got to admit that. And — and" — he sort of stubbed his tongue and dropped his eyes from mine — "and you're all the world to me, Maudie. Therefore you love me, see?" He smiled entrancingly, and it's a funny thing about this love because I felt like admitting it right then and there, but of course I didn't, though realizing that it was high time to finesse the conversation, if I wasn't going to do

183

anything so silly as falling for a boy that nobody else wanted and who was only sixteen, which happens to be my age too — except I am much older than my years in many ways.

"That's awfully cute," I said matter-of-factly. "What say we take that frying pan there down to the shore and scrub it out before the grease hardens?"

"Will I have an eternal drag with you if I do?" Dick asked, and I smiled my Mona Lisa smile.

We hadn't gone more than a few steps when I realized that this move had simply been out of the frying pan into the fire — only we were taking the frying pan along with us. There wasn't any moon, and as soon as we were outside the circle of the fire light, the night was as black as velvet and very romantic. You couldn't see the ocean, but you knew where it was from the hissing sound the waves were making — like steam escaping. And just as they broke, lines of white would run parallel to the shore like great wads of cotton batting unrolling. Sometimes a wave would break in two or three places at once and the lines of white would shoot out every which way to meet each other. A necklace of stars strung along the horizon was really the lights of garbage barges being towed out to sea.

I started to drink it all in and let my soul expand, but I was rudely brought back to earth by having Dick make a grab at me. Why is it that all men, young or old and no matter how nice they are, seem to want just one thing from a girl?

"Gimme a kiss," Dick was saying hoarsely, while clutching my arm — "OUCH!" My frantic slap had missed his face in the dark, but I kicked his shins so hard I limped for days.

"Listen to me," I said, breaking his grip on my arm, which had loosened considerably after the second kick; "what kind of a girl do you think I am, anyhow? Why, I wouldn't let a man kiss me the first night I met him, even if I was cracked about him."

"But I'm cracked about you too," Dick said in hurt tones. "I was trying to show you — "

"I didn't say I was cracked about you," I said more gently. "I said even if I was, I wouldn't, and that's not the same thing as saying I was at all."

"What?" Dick said. "What?"

"Oh, pull yourself together and give up," I said. "I'll bet you don't even know what the definition of a kiss is."

"I'll bite," Dick said.

"A kiss," I said without emotion, "is an anatomical juxtaposition of two orbicular muscles in a state of contraction."

"Great gods on toast!" Dick exclaimed in awed

185

tones. "I never heard it called anything like that before." Then his voice became pleading. "Aw, c'mon, Maudie; I don't care what you call it, it's fun anyhow."

"I'll have to take your word for that," I said firmly.

Everything was packed up and Colin was throwing sand on the fire when we came back. "Hey, where you two been?" he said fretfully. "Making me do all the work."

"We've been cleaning the frying pan," I said, waving it under his nose.

"Oh, yeah?" he said with heavy sarcasm. "Oh, yeah?" And suddenly I realized that we had forgotten all about cleaning the frying pan and it was still full of grease.

"That's my story and I'm stuck with it," I said nonchalantly. And the frying pan too, it turned out. I had to stand on the running board holding the slimy thing going back because it wouldn't pack. Dick was driving, Colin having complained that he never got a break when he drove all the time — which was just another way of saying that he wanted an excuse to hold Alix on his lap, which seemed terribly brazen to me. Those sort of things are all right when they happen accidentally, but it's almost like necking when you plan it out ahead of time.

186

Well, I had to smile quietly to myself at the look of loathing he gave Alix when he staggered out of the car when we got back. He'd found out what a double portion she was, all right, and it was me he asked if I had a golf partner for the Tournament.

"Yes," I said, smiling gently in the darkness, "I have. Dick and I — "

"Gosh, Maudie!" Dick began, all excited and pleased, but Colin butted in angrily.

"What do you want to do, Maudie, come in last?" he said.

"Why don't you challenge us sometime, Bobbie Jones?" I said in a guileless way. "You and several other people."

"Well, if that's the way you feel about it, Helen Hicks," Colin came back, "how about a two-ball foursome to-morrow morning? Alix and I'll take you over with a couple of mashies and a putter. What say, doll?" And he reached over and casually roughed up Alix's bob.

Alix gave me the most affectionate smile I had gotten all evening, and I felt a pleasant glow at getting her friendship back, even though it would only be temporary, as I planned to be swept off my feet, in spite of myself, by Colin at the end of the golf match. But if I'd ever guessed what was going to happen when Dick got into the deep trap

187

in front of the eighth green, my warm glow would have turned into a chill of foreboding.

It was lovely when we started out the next morning, and I was feeling in a rather joyous mood that seems almost smug as I think of it now. Dick was looking grim and Colin was looking placid, and Alix had on a tight skirt that made her seem to drive off the first tee with four-wheel brakes as compared to my natural free-wheeling. Just to simply state a fact, I have a gift for driving, even though I do hold a niblick a little like a shovel. To me, it is a shovel.

Colin and Dick also drove, as in a two-ball foursome both partners drive and then you pick the best one and you and your partner take turns hitting it.

Dick's drive was a beauty, except for a little hook on the end of it that did carry it just off the fairway. Colin came rushing up from where his ball lay at least fifty yards behind Dick's, and started to give Dick's really very good drive the royal oiseau. I was delighted, because it showed he was jealous of my enthusiastic cries.

"Too much right hand," he told everybody; "you got to carry the club down with your left arm — like this. Get out of the way, Maudie. It was just too much right hand. That's what gave it that hook."

"And all that distance," I remarked, with a con-

188

temptuous look at Colin's drive, which really wasn't any longer than mine; but you couldn't faze Colin. He went merrily on and ended up by talking Dick out of his putt, but I didn't say anything, and we got to the second tee and Alix made another one of her terrible drives, because she will look at her shadow instead of the ball. She would play better golf if she thought less about her figure and more about her form. Then I drove, and then Dick began making practice swings for what looked like a honey, if Colin just hadn't of been there.

"Take it back slow, with your chin back, Dick — no, back, and carry the clubhead through with your left hand — no, heck, you don't see. Carry the clubhead through — through, egg!"

Well, in the end Dick topped the drive, as who wouldn't? He gnashed his teeth and jammed his driver into his bag. I began feeling rather annoyed myself.

"You looked up," Colin said pleasantly. "You got to keep your head down if you're going to learn to play golf. Like this — " He teed up his ball and my prayers went unanswered, he hitting a good one. He turned his back on it while it was still in the air with that smug look of a person knowing any shot of his will drop right out there in the middle of the fairway.

The third is a water hole with a lake you have

189

to get over with your drive, and even though it's only one hundred and sixty yards to the green, there must be golf balls as thick as clams on the bottom of that lake. It being what is known as a psychological hazard.

"Better use an old ball," Colin said helpfully, just as Dick started to tee up with the good one he'd been using, thus getting Dick's mind on the lake, so that after he dug out an old ball he just plopped it right in.

"Lucky you used that old ball," Colin said, sticking in his tee.

By this time I was really mad, because Dick and I were partners and we were being beaten, and I hate to be beaten at anything. Thinking over my love for Colin, I began wondering whether two strong natures like ours could ever be truly happy. I love being dominated, but I can't stand being bossed around. Golf certainly does expose a person's real self.

Well, while I thought these tense thoughts, we plowed on in the name of pleasure until we reached the fateful eighth tee, with Dick and I three down, and for once Dick's drive was straight down the fairway and Colin's was in the woods. Alix and he were beating the bayberry bushes and looking behind trees, and Dick and I started down the fairway.

"Gee, Maudie," Dick said, "it feels swell to have a good drive for a change. I've certainly been lousy."

"Yes," I agreed pleasantly, "haven't you?"

"I don't get it," Dick said in puzzled tones. "I can beat lots of guys that beat Colin, but he always beats me. It gets me."

"You're such a push-over," I said as one friend to another. "Anybody could beat you that tried. Anybody that spoke English, that is." And I pensively hit my toe with my brassie. Dick bristled in a belligerent yet baffled way.

"I'd just like to see anybody try and talk me out of anything," he began, getting red, but I waved a hand.

"Would you?" I said. "Well, just look around." And having dropped these few fleas in his ear, I strolled over to my ball.

Dick's mashie shot was beautiful and straight and very high, and would have stuck on the green like a fly in molasses if it had ever got there, but it came down just about a foot short and rolled back down the bank into a sand pit.

"Darn!" I said. "That means I have to hit it out." Well, I swung and the ball just spun around while I nearly fell on my face. Then Dick climbed down in with his niblick. He took a tremendous swing and sent a bucketful of sand out on the green, but the ball only rolled a couple of feet up the bank and then rolled back down again.

"Trying to dig a cellar?" Colin asked.

This seemed to madden Dick, for he swung again without giving me a chance, and this time he topped the ball and just pushed it down into the sand.

"Martingale!" Colin said. "You looked — " Before he could even finish, Dick had sent another bucketful of sand up on the green, but no ball. "Hey!" Colin yelled, waving a club. "You'll never get out that way. Wait'll I show you." And he hopped down into the pit. Dick took another swing, missing the ball entirely, and then Colin grabbed his club. "Hey, kid, keep your shirt on and let me show you," he said.

Dick flashed me a grim smile and jerked back his niblick with one hand while with the other he knocked Colin for a pond lily, whereupon he made a darb of an explosion shot out of the trap to within about two feet of the pin. It had hardly landed when Colin jumped up and leaped on Dick's back and they both rolled over in the sand.

I was so busy drinking it all in that I never saw Mr. Preston loping down toward us from some other green until Alix shrieked and danced up and down, and then I felt myself growing pale, as I remembered that he was the chairman of the greens committee and was probably coming to raise a little bit of the hot place with us.

"What's the meaning of this outrage?" he said between a roar and a gasp, on account of being out of breath from running. "Any young hoodlum that has so little respect for the property and regulations of a golf course — " He shook his finger at Dick while panting for breath.

At that point I obeyed what I expect will be the last good impulse of my life. I guess it was the maternal instinct in me or something, but anyway, Dick was the under dog and besides, he loved me.

"It wasn't his fault, honestly, Mr. Preston," I said, giving the old goat my sweetest smile with a sinking heart. "His brother — "

"Shut up!" Dick shouted to me, while I about bit my tongue with shock. "It was me, sir. I pushed him — "

"No, sir," Colin interrupted, "I jumped on him."

"Get off, both of you," Mr. Preston ordered, "and don't let me ever see either of you on this course again till I give you permission." And with that Dick picked up his clubs and linked arms with Colin, who picked up his clubs, and with never a backward glance they walked out of my life. Alix looked wildly around and then tore after them, dragging her clubs and pleading with them all the way up the hill. Mr. Preston grunted and went back to his green, with not even a pitying look at me. Pretty soon I heard the roar of Colin's cut-out and I saw the car go down the drive. I suppose Alix was with them, but I didn't care enough to look.

I walked over to the ninth tee and I sank down on the bench where you wait for your turn to drive, and I thought about the fickleness of men. Ha! ha! I thought; ha! ha! So this was love at first sight like you read about, when two souls join and blend, and then he goes off with his own brother that he could see any day of the week, and nights too, leaving me eating out my heart on the edge of a sand trap without even a backward glance or wondering how I was going to get home or anything. Not to mention Colin leaving me flat too. Flat as a sheet of paper — blank. So that's the way this brotherly love works, is it? I thought, and then I just thought to myself, "Huh!"

I was too disillusioned to move, even though hungry — emotional strain always makes me hungry — and I hadn't the least part of an idea how I was going to get home to lunch. I just went on sitting there for hours, until finally I saw some one coming up the slope to the tee where I was sitting. It was a man in a white sweater and no hat, all alone and carrying his clubs. Some one going around alone, I thought, and in a minute I saw that he

194

was Stanley Hughes, the handsomest man that ever breathed, that all the girls were who-ha about, but had to admire from afar because he was the woman-hater type that you couldn't get close to. Leaning back, I noticed how empty the woods were, and as I watched him climbing the path and getting nearer and nearer, and looking sort of lonely, I forgot all about Dick and Colin.

Men are like street cars, I decided. If you miss one, there's sure to be another one along soon.

CHAPTER VIII

SOUTHERN MAN

My new bathing suit is a lovely sort of cream tan that when it's wet you can't quite tell where I leave off and it begins. And I look rather divine in it now that I've filled out a little up top. But what was the use of it all, I was thinking, as I walked along the beach. What a perfectly sour summer it was turning out to be, with nothing but school-boys around, since the divine Stanley Hughes who I had almost cured of being a woman hater bid me a fond farewell and went back to work. Not a real man in the place, unless you count the life guard, and he was one of those wet types that wears dark glasses in the sun and tutors people.

Davy was lying on his back with his arm across

196

his eyes and his mouth slightly open and in desperation I was just going to wake him up by pouring a little sand in it, though I'd been feeling sort of caught up on him lately, when I noticed Pauline trying not to see me. There's one time when even your best friends don't know you and that's when they've just got a new man. There he was on the other side of Pauline and being almost covered with sand I could only see a little bit of him, but that was enough. There were lumps on his shoulders where his biceps were and his hair was the type that wet or dry it still looks like hair. Davy's is the long limp kind that floats out on each wave like a mermaid or something.

"Hello, Pauline," I waved gaily and walked over.

Well, if looks could kill, I'd have dropped in my tracks, but what could she do?

"Oh, hello, Maudie," she said casually and started to roll over as though she was going to sleep. Pauline is so obvious. Her little ruse didn't work, though, because the man had opened his eyes and seen me and whereas I may have my drawbacks, it seems only fair to mention that when a person sees me, that's usually all it takes.

"Maudie, this is Mr. Moxham," Pauline said. "Mr. Moxham, Miss Mason."

Mr. Moxham uncoiled like a spring and towered

above me. "How do you do," he said in a perfectly thrilling soft Southern drawl, brushing the sand off his hand on his trunks and clasping mine — my hand, I mean. "I love you." Luckily a wave broke just then so Pauline didn't hear the last part. I collapsed weakly on the sand.

"I was wondering," I said, "did you just simply wash up in the tide, or are you somebody's Leo man? I mean, is it worth my while?"

Well, he sat down on the sand beside me and started in to tell me all about himself, still holding onto my hand, but Pauline had come to.

"Greenhead on your foot, Moxey!" she shrieked. "They give a person blood poison sometimes."

Of course he let go of my hand and made a grab at his foot.

"Dirty pool," I said over his back to Pauline. I knew with the sea breeze we were having that there wasn't a fly on the beach.

Pauline just looked at me with an air of hauteur and I could see that our lifelong friendship was practically at an end.

"Guess I missed him," Moxey leaned back, looking sort of puzzled. Men are so dumb.

Then Davy came by, and Pauline, who usually treats him like dirt, called him over. "Here I am, pretty girl," he leered, and flopped on his stomach beside her.

198

"I thought maybe you were looking for Maudie," Pauline said, pulling on her bathing cap. "Gee, that ocean looks as cold as anything. I'm going down to stick my toe in it and see if I freeze. For goodness' sake, don't anybody duck me." She gave Moxey one of those kiss-me-kid looks and ran across the beach. The first thing I knew both dumb men were tearing after her like puppies after a ball and I found myself having a great time looking at the scenery all by my lonesome.

Well, I was beginning to see that this wasn't going to be so easy when Davy, faithful unto death, came back to me, looking like somebody's bad dream with his hair all wet and hanging down over his eyes in strings. There's no use talking, a girl would have to eat an awful lot of lettuce to get excited over Davy.

"Here I am, blond girl," he said.

"So I see," I said, trying not to shudder. After all, I don't suppose it's Davy's fault his neck is so long and skinny. It's just a stage boys seem to go through.

"Well, Davy," I said kindly, wondering in a dispassionate sort of way how a person like Davy could ever have any sort of love life, "how are you?"

"I'm feeling no pain, baby," Davy said, with a faint grunt, as though he thought he was being

199

funny. "You women are all falling like leaves for Moxey, aren't you?"

"I hadn't noticed myself," I said, turning over on my stomach with quiet dignity, "falling like a leaf over anybody. Who is this Moxey?"

"He's my cousin. Mother has him to wherever we go in the summer. I guess he thinks it's a little young here after the week-day widows he played around with in Maine last year. He's pretty smooth, isn't he?"

Well, somehow the idea of Davy being a blood relative of that too perfectly superb Southern man just makes you think, what's the use of heredity after all? Davy was sitting up and pulling off his jersey to get more sunburn. You could see the skin peeling in layers off his shoulder bones, or if you wanted a real thrill, you could look at the freckles on his stomach.

"Do you know," I said gently, "I have always had a sort of loathing for Southern people ever since my great-grandfather fought in the Civil War? He used to be a drummer boy at Bunker Hill or somewhere and he never got over it."

"Huh," said Davy, "but what's that to you?"

"It's just this to me" — I sat up and untied my bandanna — "those things run in families, sort of."

Davy rolled over on his side. I noticed casually that Pauline and Moxey were coming up the beach.

"Heck," Davy said, "I didn't know you felt that way, Maud. I guess I better keep Moxey away from you. He gets sore as a boil if people talk about how it was the South's fault, with slavery and all."

Pauline was running toward us. There's no use talking, Pauline's pants have shrunk.

"It's a strange thing about a war," I said moodily, "it leaves people so bitter. Look at the last war. People are still arguing about who won it, us or France. It seems to me that so long as they saved the Belgiums, it don't matter much which did the most — there's a thing like a bug going to light on you, Davy. I suppose it knows you're peeling."

"Hi!" Pauline flopped down on her knees in front of us, while Moxey stood dripping behind her, his hands on his hips. He smiled at me fascinatingly, but I was looking the other way at the moment. I thought idly what a relief it was to have a profile that you could count on.

"Hi!" Pauline said again, stretching out her legs with the sand sticking to them. "It was swell, Maud. You and Davy should have come. The water's like soup."

"That's because of all the bodies in it," Davy laughed loudly.

"Davy!" Pauline shuddered, with a helpless pleading look at Moxey, who happened to be still looking at me in that light provocative way men

have who are used to having women think they are
wonderful; only I was still looking at the ocean.

"I thought you were going to like me," he said
in a low voice, dropping down beside me. "What's
the matter with me after the first moment, honey?
Don't I go across?"

I turned and looked at him.

"I suppose you do," I said, "if a person happens
to be thinking about you."

"Don't be mean," he said. "You're hurting my
feelings. Now, Pauline here seems to think I fit
in all right. Why don't you give me any encouragement?"

I tied the knot of my bandanna and gave him
one of my rare smiles.

"I don't usually have to," I said. "There are no
drafted men in my regiment."

Moxey slapped his wet leg and sort of roared in
joy. Pauline, who had been bickering unpleasantly
with Davy, slid toward us.

"What are you two raving about?" she said.
Davy fanned a few flies away from his stomach
and rolled over.

"I'll bet I know," he said.

"Shut up, Davy," I said, "for goodness' sake."

Well, there is nothing like a little secrecy to
throw hay on a person's peace of mind, and I knew
Davy could be trusted to fuzz over at the right

time. I stared at the sand. Davy's mouth hung open in what was meant to be a teasing smile.

"Maud hates Southerners," he said. "She is still fighting the good old Civil War. So you can't make any time with her."

"Why, Maud," said Pauline, "you don't know anything about the Civil War, do you?" It's a queer thing how your best friends always act as though they knew personally all your inner thoughts.

"My great-great-grandfather — "

"He was just a great," Davy interrupted.

" — fought in the Civil War," I went on with quiet poise, "and naturally we are all a little bitter."

"Well, but Maud," Pauline bubbled, like a spigot which everybody has forgotten to turn off, but Moxey was leaning toward me.

"What's a Yankee got to be bitter about, I ask you, honey?" he said, his drawl reminding me of the Kentucky Derby and all those other old Southern customs. "What if you lost your home and your kin, and saw your countryside plundered and burnt by a — "

"Some of your kin must have escaped," I observed, "or how did you get here?"

He turned quite red, in a delightful way.

"You're mocking me," he said, throwing sand

on my head. "Why don't you be nice to me, Yankee, when I'm a stranger in these parts?"

"Maud," Pauline burst forth, "I never heard you say one word about having a grandfather fighting in the Civil War. Why, I showed you all our collection of family portraits since the Revolution up at Aunt Deborah's and you never said one word."

"No," I said, with sweet composure, "people that rave about their ancestors always seem a little vulgar to me."

Davy made unpleasant gagging noises in his throat. Davy can be an awful foul ball at times. Moxey laughed.

"Now, listen," he said, "you tell me where you think the South was wrong and I'll show you where you're absolutely haywire."

I stood up and brushed the sand off the place where it sticks when you sit down.

"Really," I said, "do we have to fight this war all over again!"

I was honestly getting a little bored, especially as I seemed to remember hearing somewhere that it was the War of 1812 that my ancestor was mixed up in. I tried not to remember, though, because I always like to give men a feeling of friction. There's nothing keeps them interested in you like something to argue about.

"Good-by," I said. "The night is dark and I am far from home. And we're having fried bananas for lunch."

I smiled naïvely at Moxey and waved my arm at Davy and Pauline. Then I ran nimbly across the beach and jumped up on the sea wall, waving gaily at some man way down the boardwalk. Goodness knows who he was, but it always looks so sort of cute to see a girl besieged by men at every step. I heard a scuffling noise and Moxey jumped up beside me.

"Here," he said, "you're not going to leave me out in all this rain, are you? How's for letting me carry you?" He smiled down at me and I noticed for the first time that his eyes sort of sat back in his head and looked out at you with an amused air.

"Do you usually rush around carrying people?" I said happily, thinking of the dirty look Pauline was probably giving me from afar. "I'd get pretty heavy, though, after the first mile."

He laughed.

"The car, honey, over there in the road. That green gem."

It really was an entirely satisfactory car. I sank down and stared at him, fascinated.

"Can you really drive a car with bare feet?" I gasped.

"Sure," he said, "what do you suppose people

did before shoes were discovered? I believe in preserving natural instincts."

"Is that why you ride in a car?" I asked innocently. He looked at me adoringly, while backing into Mrs. Phipps' hydrangea bush.

"Yes," he said, "I need it to help me capture my woman. You didn't seem to take to me at all."

I laughed merrily and gazed out over the ocean. His hand fell upon mine lying casually on the seat.

"Don't you believe in being cordial to strangers, honey," he said in that low sort of moaning voice Southerners use to get things with, " 'specially when they're so far from home?"

"Isn't it funny," I said, "but I don't seem to remember ever meeting a stranger which called me honey? Anyhow, aren't you Davy's cousin?"

"Sure enough," he said, "are you very keen about Davy?"

"Davy is an adolescent," I said with gentle gravity, "but a very sweet adolescent."

Well, we drove around for a few hours, talking about one thing and another, until I suddenly realized that it was now afternoon and Father would probably be dragging the ocean.

"Nobody will ever know," I said, smiling up at Moxey, "how I adore this, especially the family, which probably thinks I got swept out by the tide.

I live in that yellow house with the sand dune back of it."

Well, who should be parking their frames on the porch railing but Pauline and Davy, and to my intense surprise Pauline gave me a sweet smile of friendship, just as though I hadn't wolfed her man, and asked us to come over to her place after lunch. Of course there was nothing for me to do but smile sweetly back and say I'd love to, though I knew all too well that Pauline was up to something dirty. And it turned out I was right.

Pauline's family live on the bay and ever since they got a speedboat, everybody has taken up aquaplaning but me. Personally I've never gone in very heavily for summer sports. They may be all very fine for a person's health and all, but a person with a certain amount of charm generally hasn't much time to be tearing around tennis courts or swishing around in the water on the end of a board. And, anyway, I've never been able to see anything particularly seductive about one of these outdoor girls who's in a drip half the time.

But when I saw how Pauline had fixed things that afternoon, I could see how really impossible it is to ever have any real friendship with a woman. There was me and Davy and a boy that is visiting Bill, Charlie somebody and Pauline and Moxey and Julie Purviance, who is just a little bit cross-eyed and can't swim. Well, I could see what Pauline thought was going to happen: Every one would be leaping and foaming in the water but me and Julie, who would be sitting on the float looking like duds. Julie is a sweet girl with a beautiful soul, and a black satin bathing suit with black stockings and garters. I strolled out on the float, where everybody was tearing off their sweaters and doing little squatting motions with their legs to limber up.

"Here I am, best girl," said Davy, who still had sand sticking to him from the beach; "you almost missed a great sight."

I sat down on a pile of rope without noticing Davy. I have found that it is a mistake to give him any encouragement. He is always sort of underfoot even without it.

"Davy thinks he can ride the board without the ropes," Mary said, taking some splinters out of her knees from where she'd been lying on the float, "and I'm betting he's going to get a nice bath. Who took my cap?"

"I've got it," Pauline stuck up her head. "Oh, hello, Maud."

The boat was bobbing around at the foot of some steps that went down the side of the float and shook when you walked on them. Moxey was in the boat, sticking things in the engine to make it choke. He looked up and waved his arm.

"Hello, good-lookin'," he said; "were you looking for me?"

I smiled down at him.

"I really didn't notice you weren't here," I said, leaning on the railing. He sat back on his feet and smiled mournfully.

"The same terrible cruelty," he said, "and nobody even offers to help me out down here."

"Why, Moxey," Pauline stood up and leaned over the railing, "you said you didn't need any help."

"That was five minutes ago, honey," he said, "but things are much worse now. This is a pretty sick boat."

"Sinking fast," said Davy and everybody simply nearly had a spasm, the way people do that are rather immature.

"Well, for heaven's sake," Pauline said, "the captain said everything was great. He can just come out and fix the darn thing." She ran up the steps to the house and something inside me stood up and shouted that this was my one and only chance. Julie was sitting on some life-preservers wearing a brown bathing cap with her ears outside. You couldn't get away from it: Julie was one heavy muffin. I hurried carefully down the steps.

"I bet we could fix this boat," I said. "If I start

the self-starter while you turn that wheel thing, I bet it will go."

Well, of course it did. Pauline and I have done it often, when we were out alone, but Pauline hasn't much head for mechanics — she just likes to drive the boat. In a minute we were sputtering down the bay, making lovely white wrinkles in the water just as Pauline and the captain came back to the float. Pauline began waving and beckoning and jumping around, and I turned back. After all, it was her boat.

"I guess Pauline wants to drive," I said, cutting the motor low, "or you, maybe."

"Not I," said Moxey, "I'm the aquaplane's nurse. What's the matter with you driving, angel-face? I feel safer with you."

I steered the boat in and Pauline leaped on in such a hurry she nearly tipped us all over.

"Now we can start," she said gaily, glaring at me. "Maud, I'm afraid you and Julie are going to have a pretty dull time — I hope you don't mind. Moxey, you're to be first on the board and I'll drive.

"Honey," said Moxey, lifting on the aquaplane, "I've appointed myself the aquaplane's official nurse, so I'll have to stay right here in the boat, I reckon. And Maudie's got to drive or I give it all up and play house. At heart I'm afraid of the

210

water — it goes back to the time I was dropped as a baby — and I want somebody that knows all about boats driving me along when I'm out back here doing my stuff."

"Let's all go," Mary said, in that happy dense way of hers; "all but the person on the aquaplane."

Everybody leaped on and the boat started to gently sink and make a queer strangling noise in the engine.

"Get off, you-all," said Moxey; "eight of us fit too soon in this boat. Nobody but the crew need apply."

In the end, by sitting still and looking helpless, I found myself and Moxey driving the boat. I knew Pauline would be telling everybody that I was a love pirate, but I couldn't help myself. Natural selection is a strange thing.

"You're a darn cute kid," Moxey said, sitting on the engine lid behind me as we got up speed. "What makes you so different from your buddies here?"

I palpitated all over on the inside, but I was calm on the outside.

"I guess it must be my name," I said naïvely.

He thought that was priceless.

"Now, Pauline," he said, "I've been looking her over. She's got a cute little figure all right and a good-looking pair of eyes and a way of looking at you that makes you want to hold onto your hat and get out of the wind, if you follow me. I guess she makes a heavy killing among the boys, doesn't she?"

Well, I got sort of tired listening to him put the wings on Pauline.

"You know," I said, "I'm not having as good a time as I thought I'd have." He gave a sort of roar of delight and slipped into the seat beside me and slid his arm across the back of the seat.

"You don't suppose I'd be carrying on like that unless you were the girl of my dreams, honey. When I'm talking about Pauline, I'm talking about just another girl, just a daytime sweetie."

"I'm not the girl of anybody's dreams," I said forlornly. "I'm just the person who fixes the boat."

It was very sweet, the way he comforted me and soothed my torn heart, but just then there was a loud yell, and we realized that everybody was waiting to aquaplane while we went round and round.

The most dashing thing about aquaplaning is its name. Actually, a dripping person squirms on their stomach across the end of a board which is flapping up and down and tries to pull themself up by two small ropes. Often they spill off very ungracefully and if they ever do get on their feet, they ride along, feeling very proud and exhilarated, not knowing that they are bent over in front and sticking out behind, and the wind blowing on them

212

flaps their trunks like wet skin and that doesn't add to their charm. Girls usually shout and throw their heads back in a devilish way, not being able to see their bandannas hanging limply over their eye, with wet streams of hair plastering their faces. It's pathetic how often girls think they look coy and how seldom they actually do.

Davy tried to show off by not holding on to the ropes, so I gave the boat a little wiggle and off he went. We didn't have much trouble spilling Mary Brandt and the Charlie somebody, and then it was Pauline's turn. Pauline is a good aquaplaner — if that is anything to be proud of — so I just kept the boat going nice and slow and steady and she didn't have a chance to do a thing. She started yelling and waving and I knew she wanted me to speed up and do some S turns so she could show off to Moxey, but you couldn't hear what she was saying over the noise of the motor, so I told Moxey I guessed she was scared and maybe I better slow down a little more.

I had to smile to myself. Pauline couldn't do any of her cute little tricks at this speed. She just had to trail along behind us, without skidding off to the sides or wide swings on the turns or anything, and of course Moxey was bored to death with her and turned around to talk to me. But when we had just reached the buoy and I was turning us like a baby coach full of babies, Pauline gave a loud scream and fell into the water. When she came up, she went on screaming and moaning, and of course Moxey leaped off and swam over to her.

"My finger, Moxey, my finger!" she cried and he towed her back and lifted her into the boat, which I had stopped.

Well, we had a hectic time, what with Pauline having hysterics and leaning up against Moxey, and I trying to drag the aquaplane into the boat and not run into the buoy, while Moxey pulled Pauline's finger and petted her and told her not to cry. I just laughed scornfully when I remembered how pleased I had been with life.

When we got back to the dock, everybody rushed down and nearly tipped the float over.

"Gangway, everybody," said Moxey, tenderly helping Pauline up the steps as though she had a broken leg instead of a sprained finger. "Don't fret, honey, we'll find a doctor and get a board on that hand."

He helped Pauline into Davy's car and climbed in.

"Where's a doctor, anyway?" he said, looking across the village vaguely. We all started to tell him about Doctor Gryder and Doctor Phillips and Doctor Dewees, but Pauline was saying between sobs, "There isn't a single one here; we'll have to

214

go all the way to Wildwood," and before we could burst into any shout of any kind they had gone.

Pauline says she sprained her finger on the edge of the aquaplane when she fell off. I sometimes wonder casually why she screamed first, and how did she happen to fall off, anyway, when she's the best aquaplaner in the crowd? Not that I want to be catty or anything like that.

Davy came around about nine to take me to the dance at the Boat Club. I was feeling sort of depressed about life at this point, but I managed to drag out a smile as I went down the steps.

"Here I am, best girl," said Davy; "leap in."

"Leap in where?" I said, peering into the car. Davy waved his arm.

"Here beside me, queen," he said. "I've got a heart as big as a canteloupe and it beats for you, plink-plink." He flung his leg up over the door. I was feeling sort of annoyed.

"Your heart may be as big as all outdoors," I said, "but it won't get me to sit by all that bucket of crab bait. It seems like sort of old crab bait to me."

"Aw, we'll fit all right," said Davy. "You're little."

"I may be little," I said firmly, "but I take up lots of room. And nobody is going to get me to fit in with a lot of old meat."

215

Davy groaned and dumped the bucket over on the back seat.

"There," he said, "neat and clean." There are always pieces of iron and old leather and bolts on the floor, but I don't think Davy knows they are there. A thing that never changes gets to look natural.

We drove along in silence for a while, watching the sky get dark and the moon come up over the sand bar. The road ended up on the sand dunes, and we sat there thinking and not talking to each other. It was the kind of a night that made you think of all the things you had ever wanted, without knowing exactly what they were. You could see some kind of birds flying across the path of the moon and it made you want to fly too.

Well, all of a sudden, Davy sort of huddled up against me and reached around me with his arm.

"Aw, Maud," he said, "you look just swell in that dress. You've got everybody around here beat a mile. Go on, Maud, give me a kiss, won't you?"

I drew myself gently away, thinking resignedly that isn't it queer how a person can't seem to have any high thoughts without having to protect themself.

"No, Davy," I said kindly, "I believe in keeping some things sort of sacred."

"Well," said Davy, "this could be sacred,

216

couldn't it? Come on, Maudie, aw, come on. You know I like you." He leaned against me again and I slid away. It swept over me with a shudder that I was practically sitting where the crab bait had been.

"No," I said crossly, "I won't. I think it's a dumb idea going around kissing people just because there's a moon. Anyhow, you're mussing my dress."

Davy looked awfully sulky.

"You think you're pretty high hat," he said.

"I'm not too high hat to get out and walk," I said, "unless you snap out of it. Come on, don't be an octopus, Davy."

We drove to the dance in a sort of cooler relationship, but that didn't worry me because I knew one smile would have Davy at my feet again, and when we got there I practically forgot all about him, for as we went up the steps, who should we meet but Moxey and Pauline as big as life, with Pauline's hand all wound up like a bunion.

"Hello, skipper," Moxey called out to me, "I was scared you'd ditched us for that old moon."

"We did look at it," I said. "How's your hand, Pauly?"

Pauline's face took on an expression of great suffering.

"It's sprained," she said. "Moxey was simply

too, too divine the way he stayed with me when they straightened it."

Between Moxey and me there passed a look of complete understanding, and then the music started again. I dumped my coat in the cloakroom and we went into the big room where the dancing was. All the Boat Club trophies and cups are around the wall, with some stuffed fishes and an anchor, and there are doors going out on the float. Bill Brandt was doing his Al Jolson over by the orchestra when we came in. Bill just loves to show off.

"Listen, Maud," he shouted, "this is all new. I'll do it over for you."

"It's the silliest thing," Mary whispered to me, Bill as usual being no treat to his relatives.

"Now listen, Maud," Bill was wailing:

> "My heart is like an aquaplane
>   With a girl on the slippery end;
> I give a little flip when she gets too gay,
>   Then smile and let things blend."

"Isn't that swell?"

"You said your heart was like a red, red nose last week," I said, "and the week before it was a laundry check. Doesn't it ever settle down?"

Every one laughed appreciatively, even Pauline, who was looking quite mad after the song. People began to dance and in a few minutes I felt myself being possessed by what I knew was Moxey. He looked simply divine in clothes, and his sunburn was spread out evenly, instead of striking him like lightning like Bill's and Davy's.

"Come on, sweetness," he said, "you and me for the moon and the dark. I bet we could dance out there."

We edged out the doors and tried dancing on the float, but it was pretty rough. It hardly took me a minute to catch my heel between two planks and plunge forward helplessly where I would probably have fallen in the water if Moxey hadn't caught me in his waiting arms.

"Right where you belong, honey," he said, and we vanished into the darkness across a sort of gangplank. "You've got me kneelin' at your feet."

"You aren't kneeling at my feet," I said; "you're stepping on them. I guess you don't know much about girls."

Moxey laughed softly and I could feel his arm wrapping itself around me. I looked up at the moon and thought about love entering a person's life.

"I've been seeing girls since before you grew up," he said fondly, "but I never saw one like you, honey. It sort of flusters me and I can't do my best."

He seemed to be doing awfully well, I thought, what with his arm and the fact that we were on the outer float with nothing but water around us. But I guess maybe his standard is quite high.

"Angel child," said Moxey, "when I came up North I was one lonely soul, wondering what to do with the rest of my life besides just living. I'm lying on the sand feeling as low as nothing at all, and up you come like a cherub in a white robe — "

"It was a bathing suit," I said naïvely, "and the pants were brown."

It's funny but that seemed to drive him into a sort of a frenzy.

"You divine little kid," he said, "you've got to kiss me or life won't mean shucks to me."

Well, he didn't just look like the kind of a person that sits around eating their heart out.

"I don't have to kiss you," I said, "I've got lots of people to kiss before I get around to kissing you — people that asked me first."

"That doesn't count," Moxey said. "It's who deserves it most." He tipped his head against mine and looked up at the moon. I was feeling so pleased with life — relaxed, sort of. "Honey, if you could see a little bunch of land down in Kentuck, with some old trees and a lot of sweet stuff growing over fences, and a house about the size of this float, meant just for two people, and two rocks for gateposts where we'd drive in — honey, you'd run down there with me to-night, just in your dancing slippers like you are, and we'd live happy ever after."

Well, I thought of how I thought this was going to be a dim summer, with nothing to talk about but who went to what camp, and here I find myself in the arms of a fascinating man who is proposing to me with a house already built. I thought of Pauline without bitterness and realized the gulf that separated us now that love had come into my life.

"I couldn't go all the way to Kentucky without my comb and brush," I said, leaning up against Moxey and feeling his other arm winding itself around me, "but wouldn't to-morrow be all right?"

"I guess it will," Moxey said, "if you'll kiss me to make up for waiting."

And the tragedy of it all was that I had to go home with Davy and the crab bait.

I was feeling so exalted after I got rid of Davy at the door that I couldn't go to bed and I just sat by the window in my skin and looked at the sea and the moon and the stars and thought about Moxey and love and what life really meant, and then I heard a voice calling my name from outside and there was Pauline, looking up at my window and asking me would I come down a minute."

"All right," I called softly, so as not to wake the family. "Just wait till I put something on." Poor Pauline, she had made such a play for Moxey herself, but I guessed she must suspect; Moxey had been so very attentive to me. I was thinking of what would be the best way to break the news as I went downstairs, and I decided the thing to do would be to start off apologizing and say how sorry I was and how I'd tried to head Moxey off but nothing could stop him.

"Maud," Pauline whispered solemnly, when I came out on the porch, "I felt I ought to come." And then she hesitated like a person wanting to get all the enjoyment possible out of a painful duty they are about to perform. "Yes, I think I ought to tell you. Moxey and I are practically engaged."

In that moment a little part of me died.

"I'm terribly sorry for your sake," Pauline said, positively gloating with sympathy, "but he kissed me and I think he wants to marry me."

"Oh," I said.

It was really an anguished cry of disillusionment, but to Pauline it evidently just sounded skeptical.

"But it wasn't like an ordinary kiss," she said. "When I wouldn't at first, he told me about a house just meant for two he had down in Kentucky with two —"

"Rocks for gateposts where you'd drive in. And he wanted you to run right down there in your dancing slippers to-night," I finished for her.

"Maud," Pauline whispered solemnly, when I came out on the porch, "I felt I ought to come."

Poor Pauline! her eyes were hanging out on her cheeks.

"He — he said the same things to you," she gasped. "The beazle!"

"Oh, yes," I said casually, feeling much better. "You know these Southern men; you mustn't take them too seriously — they're all a little bit polygamous. I was nice to him, of course, because he was Davy's cousin."

And suddenly I realized that a devotion like Davy's was not a thing for a girl to spurn lightly.

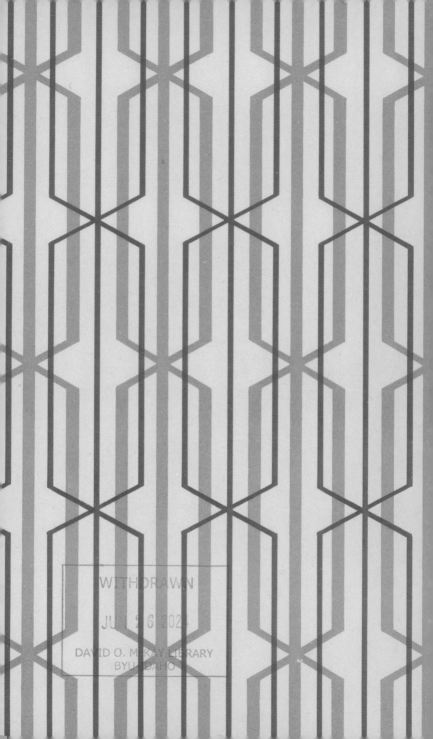